BLOOD RELATIONS

LISA TILLMAN

HILLIARD HARRIS

HILLIARD & HARRIS

P.O. Box 3358
Frederick, Maryland 21705-3358

First Edition-June 2005
ISBN 1-59133-122-6

Book Design: S. A. Reilly
Cover Illustration © S. A. Reilly
Manufactured/Printed in the United States of America
2005

For David
And my family

Acknowledgements

With heartfelt thanks to all those who helped along the way. Sharon and Mel Tillman, Ilene and Gregg Gropper, Robin and Rich Golden, Linda and Michael Manley, Alix Steier, Ron Jackson, Diane Litvak, Claudia Besen, Stuart Lowitt, Lie Ladendorf, Daryl Wood Gerber, Kadi Easly, Michelle Frankfurter, Louise Ladd, Carmen LaVia, Jan Brogan, Robin Kall, Judy Bishop, and David Frankfurter.

ONE

IT COULD HAVE been worse. At least it wasn't January.

Abigail Gardner knew from past experience that stakeouts in the middle of the winter in Boston weren't a lot of fun.

The radio on the dashboard squawked. The sound made Abby jump which isn't easy to do when your ass is numb. "He just flew by here," the voice on the other end said.

Sunk low in her seat, Abby used the van's passenger side mirror to watch as the black Mercedes took the turn into the parking lot.

"Let's go," she said. "Here comes our boy."

Abby and her camera crew jumped out of the van as the car pulled past them and parked in the row of spaces closest to the building. She moved straight for the car and was only a couple of feet away when Edward Hubert emerged from his Mercedes. As soon as he spotted the camera he started race-walking towards the main entrance of Hubert Manufacturing.

Abby sprinted to catch up with him. Alan, her cameraman, maneuvered in front of them to get a good shot. He was backpedaling furiously.

"Mr. Hubert, I'm Abigail Gardner from 'The Journal,'" she said thrusting a microphone in Hubert's reddening face. "I'd like to speak with you."

"I've got nothing to say to you people," Hubert spat.

"Why won't you talk to us about the allegations being made by the medical community about the dental drill valves you manufacture?"

"I have no comment."

"You know the valves are killing people, don't you?" Abby asked.

"That's a goddamn lie," Hubert spat.

"Medical evidence would seem to disagree."

"I have no comment," he said pushing the microphone out of his face.

"People are dying because of a product you manufacture..." Abby shouted after him.

"I have no comment," he growled as he shouldered past the camera and disappeared into his office building.

IN MOST CASES Abby hated ambushing people. It was one of the few things about her job as a television reporter that she really detested. Her employers at "The Journal," the TV news magazine where she worked, loved confronting reluctant interviewees on their doorsteps. They believed it made for great television.

Abby was all for this particular ambush, though. Hubert's company had failed to do anything about a faulty valve that they manufactured for dental drills. A recent scientific study had concluded that when the small valve malfunctioned it caused water to backup and stagnate in the drill. The authors of the study believed that the valve could be responsible for the transmission of diseases like AIDS and hepatitis, as well as bacterial infections, to dental patients. Hubert Manufacturing had refused to acknowledge any responsibility for their faulty product. She had made several requests to interview Mr. Hubert, but he had refused all of her overtures. Chasing him down with videotape rolling was the only way she could get him on camera.

ABBY NAPPED ON the flight from Boston to New York. She had flown into Boston the night before from Cleveland, and had only managed a few hours of sleep before rising at four-thirty to stake out Edward Hubert's parking lot.

Her return to the office was her first in a week and a half. She had spent four days in Cleveland on the dental drill story, and had been in Minneapolis for a few days before that. She had been with "The Journal" for four and a half years. It was a job that she loved, at least most of the time.

Not yet thirty, Abby relished the frequent travel her work entailed. She had covered stories in all fifty states, reported from Carnival in Rio, The Running of the Bulls in Spain, and the World Court in The Hague. The year before, the show even sent her to Afghanistan. She would have preferred to have covered the fighting there, but was actually dispatched to report on a series of celebrity visits to the troops.

She took a car service from LaGuardia Airport to "The Journal's" office on East Sixty-Second Street. She grabbed an extra-large coffee from the deli on the corner before heading up to the office.

"The Journal's" newsroom was a maze of grey cubicles, lit by cold, unflattering fluorescent lights. The ceilings were high which ensured that the cacophony of constant chatter, ringing phones, and blaring televisions reached everywhere. The place was always freezing, which Abby was sure was some sort of management ploy to keep everyone awake and working.

Since Abby was an on-air reporter she was accorded the much-envied perk of her own small office. The twelve-foot-by-ten-foot windowless space contained a desk, a chair, a small sofa, a phone, a computer, a television and floor to ceiling shelves filled with tapes. On the walls hung her two Emmy nominations, along with an award she received for a series of stories she did on the War Crimes Trial. Abby's favorite feature of her workspace, though, was the fully functioning door, which she closed shortly after passing through it that morning.

It took all of ninety seconds before someone was knocking on it.

"Come in."

Sigmund Lloyd, "The Journal's" Australian-born Managing Editor, stuck his head into Abby's office. His tiny, pink face was reminiscent of a rodent. His personality suggested one as well. "Welcome back, love. How did it go?"

"Pretty well."

"Great, Gordo wants to see the ambush tape in his office."

Excellent, she thought, as she picked up the tape and her coffee and retraced her steps back through the maze. There was no better way to ease back from the road to the office than with a visit to the chambers of Gordon Burrows, "The Journal's" Executive Producer. Gordon and Sigmund were part of a small battalion of Australians who in the early 1980's had helped import tabloid television to the United States. Abby couldn't imagine what Australia got in return.

A nightly half-hour program, "The Journal" wasn't a complete tabloid. It was more a hybrid--sort of a "60 Minutes" meets the *New York Post*. Abby strove for more of the "60 Minutes" end of the spectrum, but, despite her best efforts, found herself occasionally conducting interviews with people in bikinis.

Gordon's office was designed to intimidate. It was done up in a fearsome shade of gray and filled with antique weaponry and foreboding, heavy furniture. Gordon Burrows included. Abby was tall, but Gordon was off the charts. He was easily the largest human being she had ever met.

It had taken Abby a full two months of pleading to convince Gordon to let her do the AIDS Dentist story. A dentist Abby had met on a story about dangerous fillings had told her about a little-known study linking a faulty valve in certain dental drills with disease transmission. Gordon Burrows was not the type to be easily impressed with doctors and their studies.

"Boring," he had told her. "Too wordy."

"Yes," Abby agreed. "We journalists certainly don't want to get bogged down with all those words."

Gordon wanted sexy and simple. It was his credo. It was tattooed on his pickled brain. But Abby had toiled for him long enough to know how to appease him. She worked on her other stories, but continued digging. Eventually she found the beautiful young family of an Ohio man who had died from a viral heart infection that was traced to a drill in his dentist's office. The man, who was only thirty-nine, left behind a wife and three sons, the oldest of whom was thirteen. Edward Hubert was the owner of the company who manufactured the faulty valves.

"Bit of a snore, don't you think, love?" Gordon said after watching the tape Abby had shot that morning.

Abby knew Gordon would have loved it if the guy had taken a swing at her. In Gordon's eyes, the louder and more violent the confrontee's reaction, the better. Screaming humans, lunging for the camera, and/or the reporter's neck, always made for good television.

"Well, he didn't come after me with a tire iron if that's what you mean, but I think it gets the point across."

"Yes, a tire iron would have been nice, but what can you do? You can always just lose the audio, and do a track over the footage of him running away."

Sigmund nodded in agreement. "Good idea."

"I think it's an effective piece of video," Abby said, defending herself. "He clearly doesn't want to talk to me, he says 'goddamn,' and he does run away."

Gordon smiled in amusement. "Don't worry we'll figure it out in editing. How much more shooting do you have?"

"A few more days. I'm going to D.C. tomorrow to talk to someone at the F.D.A., and then I have interviews scheduled with a couple of doctors."

"Two more days?"

"Probably three."

"Good, then a week to write and two to edit. We're looking at this for sweeps."

"Terrific." Sweeps was the time of the year when the networks determined their advertising rates based on their ratings. Only the stories that would attract the most viewers aired during sweeps.

"There's a staff meeting at five-thirty," Gordon told her. "We can figure out what you'll work on next after it."

"Can't do it today. I just stopped in to drop off the tapes."

Gordon raised an eyebrow. Abby always found it disconcerting that he could raise just one. "Working half a day?"

"I've been up since four."

"And?"

"And it's my father's birthday and I have to drive up to Connecticut and have dinner with my family."

"That sounds nice."

"You've never dined with my family."

ABBY LEFT HER tapes in the care of a production assistant, confirmed her travel plans for the following day and walked up to her apartment on East Seventy-Eighth Street to shower and change. Dinner was at seven, and she was right on schedule to leave the city by five for the drive up to New Haven. She called her garage to have them bring up her car, stopped at the liquor store across the street from her building for a bottle of scotch for her father, grabbed another cup of coffee, and then went to pick up her car.

"Sorry, Miss," the garage attendant told her. "The battery is dead again. We're charging it, should be another ten minutes."

"Great." Abby said. Dinner with The Doctor, as her father was known to all who knew him, was usually a stressful enough experience without injecting tardiness into the equation. Abby could just picture her old man sitting at the table at David and Ellis, his favorite steak house, closely examining his glass of red wine in the dim light, and trying not to appear annoyed.

Abby hoped her older brother Bennett would make it there on time, but she knew better. She used her cell phone to call her father's office and left a message that she'd be a few minutes late.

The garage attendant was right, and within fifteen minutes she was on her way to Connecticut. Abby loved her car. The only reason the battery was dead was because she hadn't driven it in close to a month. The topaz blue BMW was fast, powerful, great looking and really annoyed her father. The Doctor was somewhat Amish when it came to cars. He believed they should be sturdy, reliable, safe, and definitely not built by any of the former Axis powers. Abby purchased the car on her third anniversary with "The Journal."

Luckily, the rush hour traffic on I-95 was moving and Abby made it to the restaurant by seven-fifteen. She found her father exactly as she'd imagined him: seated at his favorite table, dressed in his usual blue suit and crisp white shirt, closely inspecting the glass of red wine in his hand. Bennett was nowhere in sight.

"Hi, dad," she said with a small wave. She could tell her father was angry because he didn't stand up. She pecked him awkwardly on his cheek. "Sorry I'm late."

"Hello, Abigail, how was your drive?"

Abby didn't dare tell her father about her car trouble. She was in no mood for a lecture.

"Fine," she said handing him his gift. "Happy birthday."

"Thank you," he said, putting the package aside without opening it.

"No sign of Bennett, huh?"

"No. I assume your brother will make an appearance eventually."

The Doctor had raised Abby and Bennett alone after their mother was killed in a car crash. She died a few weeks before Abby turned five.

"I'm sure he'll be here soon. Did you get my message that I'd be late?"

"Yes, I did. Thank you for being so considerate."

Considerate like picking a restaurant two hours from my office on a weeknight? Abby thought to herself.

"Why don't we order," The Doctor said, signaling the waiter.

"I'm sure Bennett will be here soon," Abby offered.

She tried to remember the last time she had seen her brother, but couldn't. She thought it might have been Thanksgiving or maybe Labor Day. She wasn't sure. Since Bennett had no regular job to report to and access to a couple of trust funds stocked with old family money, he made a regular habit of vanishing. For the past several years they had done most of their communicating through answering machine messages and email. Between Abby's extensive travel schedule and Bennett's frequent disappearances, it was the best method they had found to keep in contact.

"We'll have the tomato salad," The Doctor told the waiter. "And sliced steak for three. I assume that's alright with you, Abigail."

Abby smiled at her father. "Fine." After all it was his birthday. Why shouldn't he get to choose what everyone ate?

"Good. If Bennett doesn't bother to show up, I can bring the leftovers home for Maggie. She'd probably appreciate it more."

Maggie was The Doctor's Labrador retriever. He got her after Bennett and Abby had moved out. She was by far his favorite child.

"How's work?" he inquired as he meticulously applied butter to a piece of bread.

"Good."

"Traveling a lot?"

"Yes. I was in Boston this morning, and I'm going to D.C. tomorrow."

"I saw that piece you did on breast implants a few weeks back. Pedestrian information, but you conveyed it well. That doctor you interviewed, though, was a moron."

"Which doctor?"

"Well, look who decided to show up," The Doctor said. "And in his Sunday best." Abby looked up to see her brother, Bennett, walking towards their table wearing jeans and a leather jacket.

"Sorry, Pop." Bennett said, flagging down a waiter and ordering a vodka martini. "I got stuck at work. Happy birthday."

"Work?" The Doctor looked stunned. "You have a job?"

Abby was just as surprised as her father, but much more tactful. "Where are you working?" she asked.

"Dante's books in New Haven," Bennett said, draping his jacket across the back of his chair.

Abby knew the place well. "That's a great store, how long have you been there?"

"About five weeks," he said.

She was impressed. Five weeks was a long time for her brother to remain focused on a job. Her only sibling somehow missed the work-obsessed gene she had inherited from their father.

The Doctor twirled the wine in his glass and looked at his son. "So, you're selling books now?"

"I'm doing some sales, and I'm organizing some readings. Interesting stuff."

"Great," Abby said.

"Well, anyway, happy birthday, old man." Bennett slid a package across the table to his father. "It's a book on the Hurtgen Forrest. I thought you'd like it."

"Hurtgen Forrest, now that was a fascinating battle."

The tomato salad arrived just in time to prevent The Doctor from launching into a World War II history lesson.

"I thought you were going to make another attempt at a college education this spring," The Doctor said after they had all started on their salads.

"I am," Bennett said smiling. "I'm taking two classes."

Abby was thrilled. "That's great."

"Which two classes?" The Doctor asked.

"Russia under Stalin and Feng Shui."

The Doctor digested this for a moment. Abby chewed her tomato. She knew what was coming.

"Feng Shui?" Her old man asked after he swallowed a bite of his salad.

"I'm interested in it."

"Of course you are, Bennett, but quantify this for me if you will: do you think your interest in Feng Shui will last as long as your interest in Marine Biology did, or is this more like your interest in Post-Impressionist sculpture?"

Bennett looked around the restaurant. "Can I smoke in here?"

"You still smoke?" Abby was happy for the subject change.

"What can I tell you," Bennett said, pulling a pack of Dunhill Blues out of his jacket. "I'm a horrible person."

Abby looked at the cigarettes. "Dunhills? Who smokes Dunhills?"

The Doctor took another sip of his wine. "No, you can't smoke in here."

"Fine," Bennett pushed his chair back and stood up. "I'll just step outside."

Abby watched her brother grab his jacket and walk out of the restaurant.

The Doctor speared another bite of his salad. "I'm assuming he won't be back."

Abby knew he was right. As far as family dinners went, this one wasn't that bad. Usually when Bennett stormed out of a restaurant he didn't go that quietly.

TWO

DESPITE THE FACT that Abby had slept only a few hours over the last couple of days, she insisted on driving back to New York after her father's birthday dinner. The Doctor, noting the late hour, had invited her to stay with him, but Abby declined.

The Doctor still lived in the house where Abby grew up. The three-story Victorian in Easton, Connecticut, had been in the Gardner family for four generations. The place was magazine-quality stunning. It had five fireplaces, a wrap around porch, and landscaped grounds that stretched to the shores of the Long Island Sound. The gardens at Chez Gardner were The Doctor's passion. When he wasn't working, he was always planting, pruning, or fertilizing something. During the winter months when his garden was dormant he would focus his energies on the house's beautiful woodwork. Floors, stairs, banisters and sills were waxed, polished and rubbed to their gleaming, rich glory. The house was like a museum, beautiful but not exactly well suited as a home for two kids.

Abby's entire apartment would probably fit in her father's living room, but she loved her place just the same. The one bedroom co-op was in a well-maintained pre-war building, and made up for its lack of size with charming details like ornate moldings and a claw-footed bathtub. She moved into the apartment right after she started working for "The Journal."

EARLY THE NEXT morning, Abby grabbed a cab right outside of her building and caught the nine-thirty shuttle to D.C. She met her crew at the airport and headed to the F.D.A. She completed two in-depth interviews by six-thirty, met a college friend for dinner in Georgetown and was back in her hotel room by eleven-fifteen. She fell asleep watching CNN and managed to get in a solid six hours of sleep before the phone rang at five o'clock the next morning.

During her years with "The Journal," Abby had gotten used to Gordon Burrows' middle-of-the-night phone calls. He enjoyed rousing people from a sound sleep in order to talk business. It gave him an edge. He could tell them what he needed, how he wanted it done, when, where and why, while they were still trying to get their eyes to focus and wondering if the phone cord would stretch to the bathroom.

Gordon used Mother Nature as his weapon. He could easily get his overworked staff to see things his way with a simple fifteen-minute phone call at four in the morning. He had learned some time ago that most people will agree to practically anything when they are desperate to go back to sleep and/or they really have to pee.

"What do you want?" Abby grumbled into the phone. She didn't bother to even open her eyes as she waited to hear what locale he would attempt to dispatch her to next. Was there a new-found serial killer terrorizing the Pacific Northwest, or had a small mid-western city recently elected a goat as mayor?

Gordon cleared his throat, and Abby got the chills. "Gordon?" She asked, opening her eyes.

"It's your father; I think you'd better come home."

Abby made it from her hotel in D.C. to the main lobby of Harborview General Hospital outside of New Haven, Connecticut in less than five hours. She'd put herself together quickly in Washington, and was in a taxi bound for the airport thirty minutes after she talked with Gordon. He'd arranged for her flight back to New York. He also arranged for the airline to get her on and off the plane as quickly as possible, and he arranged for a limo to take her to the hospital. He arranged everything. It always came as a surprise when it occurred, but every once in a while, Gordon Burrows could be positively human.

"I'm looking for my father; he's a patient, Charles Gardner," Abby told the guard at the lobby desk. He tapped a few keys on his computer. "Take the elevator to the third floor," he said pointing behind him. "Check with the nurses' station."

Gordon didn't have any information on her father's condition when he'd called her in Washington. All he could tell her was that her old man had called the ambulance himself, but was unconscious by the time the paramedics arrived. They had to break into the house to get him.

She had tried calling the hospital from the plane, but the operator had no information about her father. She called from the car as well, but was told they couldn't tell her anything.

Abby stopped at the nurses' station, and again asked for her father.

"Abigail," a familiar voice said. She felt a warm hand on her shoulder, and turned to see Helen Bishop, her father's long-time nurse standing behind her.

"Please tell me he's okay. No one will tell me what's happening."

"They think it was a stroke. He was brought in here unconscious about seven hours ago. They're doing everything they can for him."

"Is he going to be okay?" She asked, the question catching in her throat.

"I don't know."

"I want to see him."

"In a little while, sweetheart," Helen said, putting her arm around Abby and steering her down the hall. "They're still running some tests. Why don't we go sit in the waiting room? I think we'll be more comfortable, and it could be a while."

Abby only nodded and bit her lip. She couldn't speak and fight tears at the same time.

"Did you reach Bennett?" Helen asked as they waited.

"I tried him before I left Washington and from the plane, but I kept getting his machine. He'll check it eventually."

Abby thought it was classic Bennett. She's three hundred miles away, but still manages to get to the hospital first.

"I left a message earlier, too. I knew I'd have an easier time finding you. Mr. Burrow's was very helpful. He was so concerned."

"Yeah, I'll bet," Abby said.

"He told me he'd get in touch with you and have you on the next plane home, and he did."

Abby couldn't argue with Helen. She was one of the few people on the planet who Abby found it impossible to fight with. The woman had shown her nothing but kindness for the last twenty-eight years--she remembered every birthday, every graduation, every significant event--and she made sure The Doctor remembered them, too.

BLOOD RELATIONS

After about a half hour, Helen said she was going to see if there was any more information on The Doctor and walked out of the waiting room. Abby was glad to be alone. A TV set that hung from the ceiling was tuned to a morning talk show. She tried to concentrate on the chatter, but found it impossible. Her thoughts could only focus on one thing: her father's impending death.

Abby thought back to his birthday dinner and wished it had gone better. Bennett could be such a jerk. Why couldn't he just once show up on time? And why didn't she agree to stay at the house with him? She tried to recall how her father looked that night. Did he appear sick? Had he said anything about not feeling well? She didn't think so. Even if he were feeling ill he wouldn't have said anything about it. The Doctor wasn't one to complain.

"Abigail."

Helen was back, this time accompanied by a bearded man in a white coat with several white index cards in his hands. Abby thought he appeared to be there for some sort of a speech.

"This is Dr. Lang, the neurologist who's been caring for your father."

"Is he okay? How bad is it?"

The Doctor shuffled the index cards and cleared his throat. "He's stable, but it's going to take a little while for us to ascertain the full extent of the damage. We were lucky that we got him in here fast and were able to use a kind of drug called a t-PA which works to dissolve the clot causing the stroke. We have him on blood thinners right now, and we're just waiting to send him for some tests which will give us some of the information necessary to assist us in localizing the focus of the injury, which in turn will help us to prognosticate."

Abby looked at Helen.

"It will help them figure out what part of the brain was injured and how extensive the damage is," she translated.

"Can I see him?" Abby asked.

"For a moment," Dr. Lang said. "He's heavily sedated."

Abby was allowed a few minutes with her father before they took him for testing. The sight of him lying so still, with so many tubes and wires coming out of him frightened her. Charles Gardner was not a small man, but the trappings surrounding his hospital bed made him look tiny. The gauntlet of blinking machines made it appear that The Doctor was being prepared for launch.

13

Abby sat down in a chair next to the bed and took her father's hand. She held it uneasily in hers, but it did not hold hers back.

She was at a loss for words. All she could think was *Please don't die.*

When it was time for The Doctor's tests, his nurse suggested that Abby might be more comfortable in the visitor's lounge. Abby thought so, too, until she discovered "The Journal's" senior correspondent, Maxwell M. Markham, waiting there.

"What are you doing here?" she demanded.

"Abigail, love," Markham said as Abby deflected his attempt at a hug. "Gordon sent me as an emissary of sorts to inquire about your father's condition. Yours as well, of course. If you don't mind me saying so, you look like shit, love."

"Thank you."

Abby noticed that most of the people in the hallway near the waiting area were staring at them. At six-foot-four, with a pompadour that defied several basic laws of science, Maxwell Morrison Markham had that effect. And that was before he opened his mouth. Markham was the Australian who was generally credited, and/or blamed, depending on your point of view, with the creation of tabloid television. A national magazine had declared him "The Sleaziest Man in America" for three straight years.

"How is your father faring?" he asked as Abby steered him into the waiting room.

"They think it's a stroke."

Markham shook his head. "Tsk, tsk, nasty business, love. I'm awfully sorry. How bad is it?"

Abby shrugged.

Markham attempted to put a supportive arm around Abby. "Well, buck up, lass. He's going to need your strength."

Mercifully, Markham's pep talk and attempt at physical contact was interrupted by a commotion coming from the direction of the nurses' station.

"Fuck you all! I will smoke wherever I goddamn please!"

Abby and Markham stepped out into the hallway to better observe the scene. A troubled looking woman was arguing with three nurses and a security guard. She was waving a lit cigarette in their faces. The woman, who was about Abby's age, was pretty, but pale, and much too thin.

"Call a fucking cop! See if I give a shit! My fucking taxes pay for this fucking place and all your fucking salaries, and if I want to fucking smoke, you'd better believe that I fucking will."

Markham was grinning from hairy ear to hairy ear. "This is incredible, Abigail, bloody incredible! Do you realize who that disturbed young woman is?"

Of course Abby knew who she was. Every man, woman and child in the free world knew who she was.

"Emily Boyle," Abby said with disinterest. She had other things on her mind.

"Don't you fucking touch me!" The young woman shrieked at a guard who was trying to quiet her down.

"That's not just Emily Boyle, Abigail! That's Emily Boyle whacked out of her mind on something!"

Abby looked up to see a man put an arm around Emily's shoulders and whisper something in her ear. "Fine," Emily shouted as she ground out the cigarette on the floor. The man turned around. It was Bennett.

Great, Abby thought to herself. She hadn't thought the day could get much worse.

"This is fabulous," Markham cackled as he pulled out his cell phone and punched in a number. "Gordon will absolutely piss his pants. I wonder what she's doing here?"

Abby sighed. "I get the feeling she's with me."

DURING HER YEARS with "The Journal," Abby had actually done a few stories involving Emily Boyle and her clan. They were hard to avoid. Emily was the eldest daughter of the late, much loved United States Senator, Gilbert Boyle. The family, which had been a defining force in twentieth-century American politics, was considered American royalty. Scattered amongst a family of war heroes and never too closely scrutinized empire-building millionaires, were several U.S. congressmen, a couple of ambassadors, a Supreme Court Justice, and the governors of two states. With the help of their movie-star good looks, youthful vitality, and sacks full of cash, the Boyles had seduced a nation. It only added to their aura when a string of tragedies befell the family during the last twenty-five years, martyring them in the eyes of the nation.

Emily was part of the next generation of Boyles, a few of whom had elected to continue the family's tradition of public service. Most of the younger Boyles were like Emily though; content to enjoy the good life, spending the family's fortune and providing occasional fodder for the gossip column.

"Oh, it's so wonderful to finally meet you," Emily said as she shook Abby's hand. "Bennett talks about you constantly. Non-stop. All the time."

Abby found Emily's sympathetic warmth unnerving. She always respected a good mood swing, but the speed and breadth of Emily's concerned her. She believed it to be the true sign of a psychotic.

Markham had followed them into the waiting room and was on his cell phone reporting all of the action to Gordon.

"We really should make plans to get together for dinner or something," Emily said to Abby, the world-famous Boyle smile firmly in place.

Abby forced a return smile. "That would be great, but I'm not really making any plans until my father is out of intensive care."

"She means well," Bennett said under his breath.

"Of course," Emily said, trying unsuccessfully to take Abby's hand. "I understand completely."

Abby tried to move away from her, but couldn't. Ever since Bennett had ushered Emily into the waiting room she had been standing uncomfortably close to Abby. Each time Abby stepped a few inches back, Emily would rapidly recover the distance. The woman had a serious space problem.

"Ben, sweetie," she asked, reaching into her bag. "Do you think it would be all right if I smoke in here?"

"I think you're going to have to go outside to smoke," Bennett said.

"Jesus Christ, this place is like a friggin' gulag!" Emily yelled. "Haven't these people ever heard of the fucking Bill of Rights?"

Abby bit her lip and looked at her brother. Bennett looked at the floor.

Emily found her cigarettes, and gave Abby's shoulder a reassuring squeeze. "I'll be back in a few minutes. Do you need me to bring you anything? Something to eat? Coffee, tea?"

"No, thank you."

"I'll just be a few minutes," Emily kissed Bennett on the cheek, looked curiously at Markham and walked out.

Abby smiled at her brother. "She's charming. Really. It's so rare to find that special mix in a girl: good breeding and yet the ability to freely spew obscenities in a public place. You're a lucky man."

"Shut up."

"I didn't realize it was customary to bring a date to a stroke."

"Are they sure that's what happened?"

"Pretty much."

"Is he going to be okay?"

Abby shook her head. "I don't know."

IT TOOK A while, but Abby was finally able to persuade Markham to return to the office. Helen had left long ago to start rescheduling The Doctor's patients. Young Miss Boyle, however, was a different story. Abby, Bennett and Emily spent the afternoon together, waiting for news of The Doctor's condition.

Truthfully, Emily's personality fluctuations did help break up the monotony of waiting, and her and Bennett's frequent cigarette breaks proved helpful in retrieving the necessary coffee and chocolate bars from the cafeteria. But at half past four, she informed the siblings Gardner that she had a Pilates class that she "just couldn't get out of."

It took a great deal of self-control, but Abby withheld comment. She feared that anything she might say could be misconstrued by Emily as trying to dissuade her from leaving.

It wasn't until late that afternoon that The Doctor was brought back to his room. Abby and Bennett moved from the uncomfortable chairs in the patients' lounge to the uncomfortable chairs at their father's bedside.

Abby sat beside The Doctor's bed, her concerned gaze shifting from her father to her brother. Bennett couldn't seem to sit still. He'd move from the chair, to the windowsill, to the bed. Then he'd pace for a while. Then start all over again at the chair.

"How long have you been seeing Emily?" Abby asked, interrupting his pacing.

"About ten months."

"Is it serious?" she asked.

Bennett shrugged.

It didn't surprise Abby that her brother had been seeing someone for almost a year and never mentioned it. She loved Bennett, but had very little knowledge of his day-to-day life. Email and answering machines can carry a relationship only so far.

It wasn't always that way. When Abby and Bennett were little kids they were inseparable. Bennett was a devoted and protective big brother, and Abby adored him. Eight-year-old Bennett had been in the car with their mother when she was killed. They were driving home in a rainstorm when they were broadsided by a landscaper's truck that had run a red light. The driver was drunk, the car was crushed, and Abby's mother, who took most of the impact in the driver's seat, died almost instantly. Bennett was pinned in the passenger seat, both of his legs mangled. It took the fire department almost ninety minutes to free him. Bennett had spent the entire time, soaked in his and his mother's blood, pleading with her to wake up. After several operations, and years of physical therapy, Bennett's legs healed. They were never quite sure about his head. The physical scars faded with time, but to this day the psychological ones were still keeping Abby and her father on their toes.

"I'm pleased with your father's test results thus far," Dr. Lang told Abby and Bennett after their father had been in the hospital for a day and a half. "The stroke was not as sizable as we initially feared, and the damage that seems to have occurred is relatively minor. He has partial paralysis of his upper and lower right extremities and he's also having some speech difficulties."

"It doesn't sound all that minor," Abby said.

"The signs are good, but we certainly don't know everything yet. Some damage from stroke is not always immediately apparent. Memory loss, personality changes, these are all common sequelae. It's much easier for us to assess the physical damage than the mental. You and your brother may actually be the best judges of that."

Both Abby and Bennett were relieved after their talk with Lang, but Abby found the warning about personality changes unnerving.

Bennett told her not to worry. "He'd have to develop a personality first before it could change."

Abby's concerns became more acute after she took the unusual step of kissing her father goodnight. His eyes were closed and she assumed he was asleep, but when she leaned in to peck him on his forehead she was almost positive she heard him singing very, very softly. It was difficult to tell, because Abby had never actually heard her father sing before, but she could swear she could hear him quietly crooning "Some Enchanted Evening."

BLOOD RELATIONS

AFTER FOUR DAYS in the hospital, The Doctor was moved from the intensive care unit to a private room in the rehabilitation wing. Dr. Lang and his associates seemed pleased with his progress. Abby wasn't so sure. Aside from his obvious physical problems, Abby thought her father seemed somewhat off. Her concerns stemmed mainly from the constant presence of what appeared to be a smile on the parts of his face The Doctor had muscle control over. Abby's father was known to smile only slightly more often than he was known to ovulate. Compounding her worries was the fact that his grin seemed to increase when Abby and Bennett were around.

Abby knew her father had to have been a different man when her mother was alive. It would be the only way to explain how Abby and Bennett came to exist. She was sure Charles Gardner loved his children; he just wasn't sure what to do with them.

Bennett made it easy on his father by managing to get thrown out of every high school he was ever enrolled in. He went through three boarding schools as well before finally managing to graduate.

As her father's condition continued to improve, Abby began to resume her normal life, which meant going back to work. Gordon was eager for her to finish her AIDS-dentist piece. Abby loved the story and was anxious to complete it, but she was nervous about leaving town. Her fears were not unfounded; Gordon Burrows had a nasty little habit of sending people out of town for two days, and then keeping them on the road for three months.

"You'll only be gone for forty-eight hours at the most," Gordon assured her. "Just finish up the story, and then you can come directly home. I promise."

But Abby wasn't buying his assurances. "This isn't the first time you've dropped this particular load of bullshit on my head, Gordon."

"No, this time I swear it. Just go down to D.C. and finish this one up. Then I'll put you on the local detail for a spell."

Abby reminded Gordon that he'd said that before.

"I know," he said. "But this time I mean it. You have my word."

"Your word is meaningless," Abby told him. "I'll go out there, I'll shoot my stuff, and then I'll be boarding my flight home and you'll have me paged in the airport so I can go to Biloxi or Boise or somewhere to talk to some kid whose neighbor ate his dog."

"No, this time we promise," Sigmund Lloyd piped in.

"You said that last year, and I wound up on a three-month

cross-country freak-of-nature tour. I can't go."

"Listen, love, I am not a completely insensitive bastard. I understand about your father, and I grasp your desire to stay close by, but I just need you to finish up this one story. It is imperative that we have it for sweeps."

"Absolutely not," Abby said. She insisted that she wasn't going anywhere.

Despite her protests, Abby found herself on a plane headed to Washington the following afternoon. She had spent her morning at the hospital with her father, her brother and Emily. Bennett told her not to worry and swore he'd call if anything happened.

Bennett seemed to be relishing the newer aspects of his father's personality. When Abby left for the airport her brother and father were performing the balcony number from *Evita* for Emily. Abby was surprised by the amount of time her brother was spending at the hospital, but she knew it wouldn't last. Bennett would eventually get bored of caring for their father and disappear.

ABBY'S INTERVIEWS WENT well. She spoke to two doctors at the National Institute of Health about the dirty dental valve theory on viral transmission. She shot plenty of background footage of white-coated scientists working in laboratories, lots of test tubes, flasks, microscopes and such which would be essential for editing the story.

She called her father's room on the way back to her hotel that night and was surprised when Emily answered the phone.

"He's sleeping," she told her, her voice barely a whisper.

"Where's Bennett?" Abby asked.

"He went out to get us some dinner. He should be back in ten or fifteen minutes."

Abby asked her if they'd been there all day.

"No," Emily told her. "We left in the afternoon when he was in therapy; we came back so he wouldn't have to eat dinner alone. Do you want me to have Bennett call you when he gets back?"

"He doesn't have to. It seems like you have everything there under control."

"Don't worry, everything here is fine. Your dad had a pretty good day. The physical therapist said he's making real progress."

"Great, tell Bennett I'll speak to him tomorrow."

Abby had to hand it to Emily. For a world-famous spoiled brat she was really hanging in there.

Abby spent the next day deep in the suburbs of Virginia talking with the doctor who had published a recent paper on the faulty dental valve theory.

Dr. Felix Weitzman looked like a cartoon of a mad scientist. He was short with a shock of bushy white hair that appeared to have last been brushed sometime prior to the dawn of the nuclear age, and a huge white moustache. He sported a blue Washington Wizards sweatshirt over a white shirt, a red polka-dotted bow tie and baggy brown pants. He capped off the ensemble with a pair of rubber flip-flops.

When Abby had called to reschedule the interview with Dr. Weitzman she'd told him about her father's stroke. He seemed genuinely concerned and proceeded to spend the first fifteen minutes of their time together questioning Abby about her father's condition and the care and treatment he was receiving.

At eighty-one, the Hungarian-born Dr. Weitzman was still as sharp as ever. He was considered a pioneer in the field of hematology, and agreed with the theory that blood-borne viruses could be transferred from human to human through a faulty valve that caused blood and water to stagnate in standard dental drills.

"I hope your father's recovery will continue unimpeded," Dr. Weitzman told Abby after the interview was finished. "You will let me know if I can be of any further assistance to you?"

"I will," Abby said as the crew packed up the camera gear.

"I enjoy your show immensely, Ms. Gardner," Weitzman told her. "At least some of the time."

Abby laughed. "I feel the same way."

"That Markham fellow, though; he seems like a real pip."

ABBY WAS PLANNING to spend only one night in D.C., but the interview with Dr. Weitzman took longer than expected, and she wound up staying for a second night. She was exhausted when she got back to her hotel, and actually fell asleep before eleven.

Her sleep was fitful at best. She was so nervous about being away from her father that when the phone rang at a quarter to five she almost hit the ceiling.

"Bennett?" she asked, picking up the phone. "I knew I never should have left."

"Abigail, love, it's Gordon. Don't worry, your father is fine."

Abby's heart stopped pounding. "This better not be about another story."

"I wish it was."

Abby sensed the hesitation in his voice. Panic crept back in. "Why? What's wrong?"

"It's your brother."

"Bennett?"

"He's in jail."

"Oh, please," Abby said, more annoyed than concerned. This wasn't Bennett's first tangle with the law. "Now what did he do?"

"I think you'd better come home."

"Why? How much trouble did he manage to get himself into this time?"

"I'm afraid quite a bit. The police are calling it murder."

Abby laughed. "Murder? Funny, Gordon."

"It's not a joke. Emily Boyle is dead, and your brother has been arrested for killing her."

THREE

GORDON HAD WARNED Abby to be prepared. "The story was all over the bloody news."

He wasn't exaggerating. Abby watched television in the airport while she waited for her flight back to New York. The only story on the news programs that morning was the death of Emily Boyle. The networks had reporters stationed at Emily's apartment, the hospital, a few of her family's homes and Sussex County Police Headquarters where Bennett was being held.

It took Abby close to two hours to get from the airport to the police headquarters in Connecticut. It was obvious she was in the right place as the parking lot was lined with television microwave trucks. She knew that Bennett's name was already out in the media, but didn't know if the reporters waiting in the parking lot, many of whom Abby knew personally, would connect her to him. As soon as she stepped out of her taxi it became apparent that they did.

The first reporter to spot her was Polly Walsh from Channel Eleven. She sprinted towards Abby, microphone in hand, shouting "Abby, have you spoken to your brother?" The rest of the press corps followed. She recognized Peter Isher from Channel Five, Leslie Fuller from "The Report," and Stu Marrin from the *Daily News*. Don Cantrell, who used to be with "The Journal" and now worked for one of the cable networks, was there, too. Abby had spent time with these people--jostling for space at news conferences, waiting outside courtrooms for verdicts--they were colleagues, but that didn't seem to matter. She was the quarry now.

"What's he told you?" someone shouted as camera flashes popped.

"What was his relationship with Emily?" another one yelled.

Abby ignored them all and ducked into the building as fast as she could. She took the elevator to the second floor where the police officer behind the front desk was unimpressed with her demands to see her brother. He told her to have a seat and mumbled an assurance that someone would be with her shortly.

Abby used her cell phone to call Gordon to see if he had any further information.

"Nothing concrete, love, but we're scrapping today's program and going with this."

"Terrific," Abby said. She surveyed the scene in the parking lot from the second floor window. "I assume you won't be the only one. There must be fifty reporters here."

"Fifty-one if you include yourself."

"I'm not here in a professional capacity."

"Of course you're not, love, but you are on the inside, and if you do happen to come across anything of interest..."

"Give me a break," Abby said.

"Have you seen him yet?"

"I'm waiting to."

"After you do we'd like an interview," Gordon said.

"I'll bet you would."

"Abigail, we're covering this story, and you've got the inside scoop. We'll have the edge over everyone. Do you have any photos of your brother in your office?"

"No," Abby said recoiling at the thought of Gordon or Sigmund pawing through her things in search of a family portrait.

"You'll get us some later. Call me after you speak to him."

Gordon hung up before she could even respond. Abby planted her rear end in a blue plastic seat that was bolted to the floor and began yet another wait.

She could picture exactly what was going on in the newsroom right now. The place would be buzzing with energy. Reporters, producers, associate producers and their various assistants would be scrambling like mad trying to put together something for tonight's program. Stories were being set up, footage gathered, crews dispatched. Gordon probably pulled everyone in the office off of what they were doing to work on it. Abby loved the rush of breaking news, the frenetic pace, especially on a huge story like this.

Abby's pace in the police station however was far from frenetic. An hour and a half later she was still waiting. Removing her numb posterior from the chair she had been sitting in, she walked over to the window and stretched. Even for Abby the scene in the parking lot below was amazing. During the time she'd been waiting the reporters, photographers and microwave trucks had multiplied.

"Nothing like a second degree murder charge and the ensuing media circus to get your morning off to a running start, eh, Abigail?"

The voice was familiar. Not welcome, but familiar. Abby hesitated before turning around. She wasn't a strong believer in the concept that things couldn't get any worse.

Abby turned to find her uncle, Stanley Seaton, surrounded by three official-looking men in charcoal pinstriped suits. Uncle Stan wore his usual custom-made, double-breasted, dark blue suit. His hair was grayer than Abby remembered, but was still combed over and shellacked to his bald spot, which, Abby noticed much to her enjoyment, was getting larger. His shoes were highly polished wing-tips with covert elevator lifts inside. Stanley Seaton was a big man only in his mind. To most of those who knew him, he added new dimension to the word twerp.

"What the hell are you doing here?" Abby demanded.

"Now, now, Abigail," Stan said giving her shoulder a supportive squeeze. "At a time of family crisis like this, where else would I be?"

"Well, gosh, Uncle Stan, my father had a massive stroke last week, but I don't recall seeing you at the hospital."

"Abigail, please. Now is not the time to quibble. Bennett needs our help."

"Bennett needs my help," Abby said. "He'll do just fine without yours."

"Actually, Bennett seemed quite grateful for my assistance."

Abby was incredulous. "You've seen him?"

Stanley Seaton smiled at his niece. Abby wanted to kick his teeth down his throat.

"I've been waiting here for almost two hours," Abby sputtered. "How the hell did you get in to see him?"

"Abigail," he sighed, "I do have a bit of pull around here."

Uncle Stan had pull in a lot of places. He was the well-dressed, dirty little family secret the Gardners didn't talk about. The Doctor had tried banishing his late wife's younger brother from their lives years ago, but every once in a while, when it suited his needs, Stan would ooze back in. He was a pathological liar, Olympic caliber sycophant and all-around unpleasant specimen of the human form. He was also a sixth-term United States Congressman representing Connecticut's fifth district. Since she had turned eighteen, Abby had voted against him every chance she got.

Stan told Abby he met with Bennett and his lawyer.

"He doesn't have a lawyer yet," Abby said.

Stan grinned. "As a matter of fact, he does. I brought him one."

The thinnest-lipped of the charcoal-suited men stepped forward. "Abigail Gardner," Uncle Stan said, putting his arm around the man's shoulder. "I'd like you to meet your brother's attorney, Boyd Cates."

Cates' extended his hand. "Pleased to meet you," he said.

Abby didn't shake it. She wanted both of her hands free at all times in case an opportunity presented itself for her to wrap them around her uncle's throat. "I'd like to see Bennett," she said through clenched teeth. "Right now."

"Well, Miss Abigail," Stan said. "Why don't you talk with Boyd for a few moments, and I'll see what I can do to arrange a little visit with your brother."

Abby disliked Boyd Cates from the start. He spoke through his nose, was a friend of her Uncle's, and wore ugly shoes: loafers with both fringe *and* tassels.

"I expect the Grand Jury will hand down an indictment tomorrow at some point," Cates said as he fiddled with his blue and maroon striped tie. "Your brother will probably be arraigned the following day. At that point we will enter a plea of not guilty and we will request a low bail."

"Good," Abby said. It was the first thing she'd heard all morning that made any sense.

"Of course, he won't be released on bail," Cates said. He seemed to be concentrating on a pulled thread on his tie.

"Why not?" Abby asked.

"Ms. Gardner," Cates said as if he was talking to a small child. "I assume you are aware of his previous arrests?"

Abby was well aware of her brother's criminal record. He had been arrested five years before for buying a dime bag of marijuana.

"For that they'd refuse bail?" Abby asked.

"Normally, no," Cates said, giving up on the thread and smoothing his tie. "But when you combine it with second degree murder charges and access to unlimited funds, the district attorney takes notice."

"He's not going to flee the country," Abby said.

"Your assurances not withstanding, the court will think he's an excellent risk for flight."

"But you can't leave him in jail," Abby said. "They'll kill him in there. Why can't he just surrender his passport?"

Cates sighed. "To be quite frank, Ms. Gardner, I think your brother will be better off behind bars."

"You can't be serious."

"My reasons are twofold. One, if he remains in custody he'll be under twenty-four-hour guard. Which at this point, considering your brother's state of mind is probably for the best."

"And second?"

"I assume you realize that the magnitude of the crime your brother has been accused of is only eclipsed by the identity of his alleged victim. It's going to generate some very strong feelings."

"Your point being?" Abby asked.

"From the time she was born, Emily Boyle has been loved and admired by a great number of people, both in this country and around the world. Frankly, Ms. Gardner, her murder has angered a lot of people. Your brother might be safer in jail."

WHATEVER CONGRESSMAN Bennett pulled, worked. Within half-an-hour Abby was seated across a wooden visiting room table from her brother. A police officer stood near the door.

"Well," Bennett said, taking a drag of his cigarette and exhaling the smoke towards the ceiling. "My week is certainly beginning to suck. How's yours going?"

"You want to explain this one to me?"

"Well, Emily is dead, and the police think I killed her."

"Thank you," Abby said. "That part I know. What the hell happened?"

"I don't know," Bennett said rubbing his chin.

Abby thought her brother looked terrible. His eyes were red from crying and his lip was swollen and split. Abby noticed several fresh scratches on his unshaven face. "What do you mean you don't know?" she asked.

"Did you meet my lawyer yet?" Bennett asked. "Fun guy, huh? Did you check out his shoes? Like the fringe wasn't ugly enough, he needs tassels, too?"

"What do you mean you don't know?" Abby asked again.

"I don't know," he said stubbing out his cigarette. "I don't fucking know. We were fighting all night; I couldn't get her to leave me alone. I was tired, so I went to sleep and when I woke up around midnight she was asleep. I was hungry, so I went out to get a couple of burgers and when I got back, I couldn't wake her." Bennett ran his hands through his hair and Abby could see more scratches stretching up his arms. "They think I killed her. Isn't that unbelievable? They actually think I killed her! I loved her."

"I know you did."

"Are you going to tell Dad?" Bennett asked.

Abby hadn't figured out what she would tell her father. "I was sort of hoping to wait on that," she told him.

"Doesn't he have a TV in his room?"

She realized her father might already know. "Terrific, maybe now he'll have a coronary to go with the stroke."

"I didn't do this," Bennett told her.

"I know that."

"Yeah, well, you may be the only one."

FOUR

"ABIGAIL!" THE DOCTOR shouted when Abby walked into his room. She found it easy to understand her father when he said her name, but the rest of his speech wasn't as clear. She puzzled over the second part of his sentence before what he had said became obvious. He had asked her when she had gotten back.

"Early this morning," Abby said, leaning over and kissing his forehead. The side of The Doctor's face that was unaffected by the stroke conveyed joy at the very sight of his daughter. Charles Gardner's new-found enthusiasm for his children made Abby edgy. She wondered if it was something that he always possessed, but had kept well hidden, buried in the deep reaches of his mind, waiting for a stroke to knock it loose.

Abby had run into Dr. Renay, the squirrel-like physician in charge of her father's rehabilitation, on her way in to see her father. According to him, The Doctor had spent most of the day in therapy and hadn't heard the news yet. Abby was almost hoping he had, it would have made her job easier.

"I was in a quandary as to whether or not to tell him myself," Dr. Renay told Abby as he ate raisins one by one out of a small box. "I held off for most of the day hoping that you would eventually arrive to do it yourself. It's been my experience that patients deal better with unpleasant news when they hear it from a family member."

"I was in Washington when I heard," Abby apologized. "I've been dealing with my brother all day. I got here as fast as I could."

"I'm sure you did," he said, peering into the small box to see if he had indeed finished all of the raisins. He found one more and popped it into his mouth. "I'd advise you to just tell him the basics for the time being. He might have trouble digesting too much information at once."

"I only know the basics myself at this point."

"Just take it slow."

Slow had never been Abby's preferred speed.

"Listen," Abby told her father. "There is no easy way to say this, and there's going to be no way to keep it from you, so I am just going to say it. Bennett's girlfriend Emily is dead."

Abby could see the part of her father's face he had control over tremble. Most of his words were garbled, but three were clear: "That poor girl."

"And Bennett's been arrested for killing her."

"What?" he shouted.

Abby started inching towards the panic button on the side of her father's bed. "He didn't do it."

"Of course he didn't do it," he slurred. "We've got to help him."

Abby told him that Stan had arranged for a lawyer.

"That son of a bitch! What does he want?"

"I haven't figured that part out yet."

ABBY PICKED UP moo-shoo chicken and vegetable fried rice on her way home that night and ate it in front of the TV. The death of Emily Boyle was, of course, the top story everywhere that evening. Abby knew nothing short of the re-eruption of hostilities in the War Between the States could have bumped this particular story from the opening of every newscast.

As a journalist, Abby was uncomfortable with stories that began "sources tell us" or "unconfirmed reports claim," but that was what the bulk of the news programs had to offer their viewers that night. The reports all began with the facts--both of them--Emily Boyle's death and Bennett's arrest, and then plunged onward and information-less from there. Once the newscasts had exhausted all of the available gossip, rumors and supposition, they hauled out historical footage and told the always-engrossing tale of "The Boyles of America."

Emily's great-grandfather, Wilson Banion Boyle, was one of the famed robber barons who made their fortunes with the railroads. He was well known for his low wages, high rent and belief that indentured servitude had some good points. His interest in politicians was limited to the ones he had actually purchased, including his two brothers, Godfrey, a United States senator and Samuel, a federal judge.

Wilson Boyle married late in life and had two sons. His boys took a much more benevolent view of politics, which is easy to do when your old man built the railroads. Wilson Jr. and Gilbert Boyle each spent a great deal of their father's money on getting themselves elected or appointed to power.

Wilson Jr. served unremarkably in the New York State Assembly for twenty-eight years. His undistinguished service was only notable because the length of time he spent in the legislature doing almost nothing. His major accomplishment during his extended tenure in Albany was shepherding through a bill establishing three state-owned golf courses in Westchester County.

Gilbert Boyle took over his father's business interests and quickly discovered that Junior Robber Baron was not a career easily melded with elected public service. After an early disappointment in a heated congressional race, Gilbert realized he was destined to make his mark in politics by continuing his father's tradition of exerting economic clout in the political arena. His generous support, however, was rewarded with a stint as the U.S. ambassador to Belgium.

Gilbert Boyle Jr. was the first of Wilson Boyle's grandchildren to enter national politics. He was elected to congress in 1960 after a massive campaign financed and orchestrated by his father. Gilbert Boyle Sr. was going to see to it that his son would have the brilliant political career that he was denied. The United States House of Representatives, he insisted, was only the first step.

Gilbert Boyle the Younger was genetically engineered for success. Handsome, young and rich, his election to congress and the family that put him there made him a natural focus for the national media. The year after his election, he seized the country's attention when he married Anne Leland, the socialite daughter of cola magnate Harrison Leland. The wedding was featured in *Life* magazine, and their son, Thomas Wilson Boyle, was born the following year. Gilbert III followed soon thereafter.

Anne campaigned vigorously for her husband's re-election with both boys in tow. The dashing young congressman was often photographed with his beautiful wife and his young children sailing, swimming or just lounging around looking fabulous. The nation adored the Boyles, and Gilbert Sr. believed that his son's potential was without limit.

The Boyle's first daughter, Emily, was born two months after Gilbert Boyle Jr. took the oath of office as the Junior Senator from New York State. In 1970 Anne became pregnant again, but died while giving birth to a second daughter, Cassandra. Her death was only the first in a series of tragedies that would forever enshrine the young family in the hearts of most Americans. Three years later, the country grieved with the family again when ten-year-old Gilbert III was killed after being hit by a car.

Senator Boyle's pain was felt by a nation. A vocal and angry critic of the war in Vietnam, he threw himself into his work. As a member of the Senate Foreign Relations Committee he made several trips to Southeast Asia during the early seventies.

It was on a P.O.W. fact-finding mission to Vietnam in 1974 that the Senator was killed in a plane crash. His wife's mother would raise his three surviving children.

When the reporters finished with the story of The Boyles, they told what they knew of Bennett Gardner. They said he was thirty-one, and the wealthy nephew of powerful Connecticut Congressman Stanley Seaton. They said that he had a record, but few mentioned it was for minor offenses. They said he floated from job to job. They showed his apartment building and a couple of the more enterprising reporters even sought out the impressive looking house where Bennett grew up. They didn't know much, but, for the most part, that didn't seem to stop anyone.

FIVE

"What?" Abby grumbled when she answered the phone at a quarter to six the next morning.

Gordon Burrows cackled into the phone. "So, you're Stanley Seaton's niece? Christ, he ever disgusts me."

"Well, that's certainly an impressive achievement," Abby said. "I'm sure he'll be thrilled when I tell him."

"I can't believe you never told us you were related."

Abby told very few people Stan Seaton was her Uncle. "It's considered sort of an old family secret--like syphilis."

"Weren't they investigating him for influence peddling, or racketeering or something?"

"There were some questions a few years ago about his campaign finances, but nothing they could prove."

"Right," Gordon laughed. "That was it. Cash donations."

"Is there something you wanted?" Abby was in no mood to go over her Uncle's résumé.

Gordon asked her how she was holding up and Abby was immediately suspicious. "What do you want?" she asked.

"Just wanted to see if you had any interest in doing an interview?"

"Not at the moment."

"How about your brother?"

"Are you kidding me?"

"You will give us an exclusive when you do decide to talk, right?"

Abby rolled her eyes. "Yeah, Gordon, as soon as we decide to talk, we're all yours."

"THEY WANT ME to plead."

"And *they* are?"

"Uncle Stan and that lawyer person."

Abby was back in the visitor's room of the Sussex County Jail. The walls of the tiny room were white-painted brick, and the place smelled of stale cigarette smoke.

"When did you see them?" Abby asked.

"You're my third visitor this morning."

Abby looked at her watch; it was only ten after nine. She guessed her uncle didn't have to stick to the posted visiting hours. "Great," she said.

"They said the medical examiner thinks she was beaten to death," Bennett said.

Abby knew all about the preliminary autopsy results. Markham had procured a copy of the report before the coroner's table had been hosed down. She knew the toxicology reports weren't in yet and she knew the medical examiner that conducted the autopsy had noted a surprising lack of contusions on Emily's body.

Bennett lit a cigarette. "They said the district attorney really wants this to go away."

"I'm sure he does. What did you say?"

"I said I didn't do it."

"And?"

"They didn't seem impressed."

BOYD CATES WAS right about the grand jury. They did meet that morning and they did hand down an indictment charging Bennett Gardner with murder in the second degree in the death of Emily Leland Boyle. They also included a charge of felony murder, a crime that in Connecticut carries the maximum penalty of death by lethal injection.

BENNETT'S ARRAIGNMENT WAS scheduled for two o'clock the following afternoon. By the time Abby got to the courthouse, every newsgathering organization on the planet had set up camp. All of the networks and the news channels were planning to interrupt their regular programming to carry it live. Made-up daytime drama was about to be preempted by the real thing.

In addition to the news crews, a large number of spectators had turned out to gawk at the goings on hoping to catch a glimpse of

Emily Boyle's relatives or those of the handsome young man accused of killing her.

After Abby pushed her way through the crowd outside of the courthouse, she had to fight to cut a path through the members of the media waiting inside. She couldn't see Markham, but she knew he must be there somewhere. Questions were coming at her from every direction, but she ignored them all as she barreled through the gathered mass of reporters and microphones with fierce determination and the assistance of a sympathetic cameraman she knew from work. The cameraman, Jon Rosen, was the size of a small yeti, which made it simple for him to clear a trail for Abby as he walked backwards through the crowd videotaping her. He gave her arm a supportive squeeze as she passed by him and made her way into the equally packed courtroom.

Reluctantly, she took a seat next to her uncle and his security detail in the second row of the courtroom. She didn't like it, but she knew they were the only way she was getting out of there.

Across the aisle from Abby and her uncle sat Thomas Boyle, Emily's older brother. A lawyer with the attorney general's office in Washington, Thomas had inherited his father's chiseled features and mop of thick, dark hair, which he seemed to be constantly pushing off of his forehead. He was also heir to his father's political aspirations. He was rumored to be planning a run for the U.S. Senate. Forty-one and single, he often topped magazine lists titled "Sexiest Man With A Brain" and "America's Most Eligible Hunks." *Newsweek* had recently profiled him as part of an article on people to watch.

At ten minutes after two, Bennett was escorted through the side door of the courtroom by two deputies who would stay by his side throughout the entire proceeding. Boyd Cates barely looked at Bennett, but Abby couldn't take her eyes off of her brother. He wore a bright orange prison jumpsuit and stood with his hands cuffed behind his back. Abby could tell from the added bulk under his clothes that he was wearing a bulletproof vest. The thought of it made her chest hurt.

The Honorable Elizabeth J. Gower presided over the proceedings that lasted for all of two hundred and forty seconds. The judge looked none too pleased with the amount of press this particular case had attracted.

Bennett, Cates and the assistant district attorney all stood as the judge read the charges against Bennett to the court.

"At this time does the defendant wish to enter a plea?" the judge asked.

"Not guilty, your honor," Boyd Cates answered.

As Cates had predicted, the prosecutor asked that Bennett be held without bail and the judge agreed.

Four minutes of court proceedings begot hours of press conferences. Boyd Cates' was relatively short, the prosecutor's wasn't. And for the first time in her life, Abby saw her uncle, the congressman, walk away from television cameras.

Scores of reporters shouted questions in Abby's general direction as she exited the building. Stan's goons formed a hairy, protective fence around her. They got her out of the courthouse and into her car.

Abby headed out to see her father. Dr. Renay managed to stop her before she made it to his room.

"We kept him in therapy during the arraignment," he informed her. "People are, of course, discussing it here, but the staff has been forewarned about talking about the case in front of your father. They are professionals and I don't think we will have any problems."

"Good," Abby said as she headed towards her father's room.

Dr. Renay trailed after her. "I considered turning off the television service to his room."

"Why?" Abby asked without slowing down.

"I don't want to cause him any additional stress."

Abby stopped to face him. "And I do? Look, my father knows my brother has been arrested. He knows the charges against him. He also knows Bennett is innocent. I'm not planning on keeping anything from him. You people keep assuring me that his intellect was unaffected by the stroke."

"True, but..."

"I wouldn't withhold any information from him. He'll get upset if he thinks he's uninformed."

"STAN MAKES ME nervous," Abby told her father.

"He makes me nauseous."

Abby sat with her father as he ate his dinner. She felt an uncontrollable urge to help him as he struggled with the rainbow-colored assortment of pureed foods on his tray. But she feared his reaction if she did.

"What about this Cates?" he asked. The Doctor was still slurring his words, but Abby thought either she was getting more adept at understanding him, or the speech therapy was working.

"I'm not sure."

"What did Chester say about him?"

At her father's request, Abby had called his personal attorney, Chester Randolph, to check up on Boyd Cates.

"He said he isn't exactly up on who's who in criminal defense, but he'd ask around and get back to me."

Abby didn't bother telling her father that his old friend sounded like the last thing he wanted was anything to do with the Gardners and their lurid legal hassles.

Father and daughter watched the evening news together, much like they had when Abby was growing up. Abby kept one eye on the television and one on her father. She didn't want him getting aggravated. Both eyes were focused on the screen, though, when an expensively dressed young woman who looked a lot like Emily Boyle was interviewed outside the courthouse after the arraignment.

"Bennett Gardner is an animal," she said dabbing at her nose with a tissue. "And Emily was terrified of him."

The woman was identified as Gwendolyn Mason, a longtime friend of Emily Boyle.

"Bennett always pretended to be this romantic, poet-type, which Emily really went for, but I never bought it. I always thought he was a pig."

Ms. Mason explained that she met Emily Boyle at summer camp when they were both nine. "Emily was like a sister to me," she sniffled. "She was the one I turned to during my divorces. I'd been staying with her on and off since the last one--as long as Bennett wasn't around. He knew I didn't like him, so if he was there, Emily would ask me to leave. It was like she was under a spell when she was around him, she'd do anything he said."

She told the reporters that the last time she saw Emily was a couple of days before she was killed. "I had gone over to her place to pick up some things that I had left there, and we wound up hanging out for a while. We just sat around and talked, but as the hour got late she started to get nervous. I asked her what was the matter and she told me she wanted me to leave before Bennett came over. She said she was sorry, but that he would flip out if he found me there. The poor thing was really terrified of him."

AFTER THE HOSPITAL, Abby took a ride to The Doctor's house. He had asked her to retrieve several books for him and to make sure everything there was okay. Abby was happy to do it. She was anxious to find anything that would keep her from watching the news all night.

Easton, Connecticut, sits on the shore of the Long Island Sound, a scant few miles from New Haven. It was the kind of quaint place often pictured in commercials for adult protein drinks or granola-based breakfast cereals. Abby had fled the town the first chance she got.

She was sixteen when she left for college. While most kids her age were beginning their junior year of high school, Abby was starting her freshman year at Columbia University. She knew her father was disappointed that she had chosen Columbia, as he had barely spoken to her for the month before she left for school. Five generations of Gardners had attended Yale, and The Doctor couldn't understand why Abby refused to continue such a long standing tradition.

Before going in, Abby took a drive past her father's house. Knowing the press the way she did, she suspected someone might be watching the place, and she was right. There appeared to be two reporters staking out the house from across the street. She avoided them by parking at the public beach two blocks away and walking back along the shore. She cut through several neighbor's yards to make it to the back door.

Abby emptied the sand out of her shoes on the back steps and let herself in. She had learned early in life that sand, along with all other forms of dirt and disorder, were not welcome in her father's home.

The answering machine on her father's desk was blinking. The computerized voice told Abby he had thirty-seven messages. She listened to them as she gathered the books The Doctor had requested. The calls were equally divided between news organizations seeking interviews and borderline psychotic citizens calling to tell The Doctor what they would like to do to him and his son. The press phone calls didn't surprise Abby and, in truth, neither did the threats. She made a mental note to change her father's phone number first thing in the morning.

Abby got back to her apartment in time for the late news and discovered that congressman Seaton's camera shyness at court earlier that day was only a temporary condition. He wanted to talk to the press, but on his own turf.

Seated on his cream-colored living room couch, the cardigan-sweatered politician spoke lovingly of his wrongly accused and deeply misunderstood nephew. He told the world about the bevy of problems that had plagued Bennett since childhood, beginning with the death of his mother when he was eight, which had continued to haunt him throughout his life.

Abby's head began to swim as childhood pictures of Bennett and the family began to appear on the screen. Uncle Stanley spoke about the numerous schools Bennett had been ejected from for discipline problems, as well his troubles with alcohol and drugs. She was stunned as photographs of her mother--Stanley Seaton's dead sister--began to flash on the screen as well.

"Oh, my god!" Abby shouted at the television. "He gave them pictures of my mother."

Abby knew she had done this hundreds of times herself. Television, after all, is all about pictures. *Are there any photographs?* she would ask on story after story. She had begged, borrowed and bought hundreds of them over the years.

It will help tell the story, she would promise. *It will help draw the viewers in,* she would plead. *It will have more of an impact. It will be more sympathetic. It will make people angrier. It will help drive home your loss. It will be whatever it takes for you to let me have your family album so I can show it to the world.*

And there they were now, in some sort of grand cosmic revenge: photographs of her family, of her brother, of her childhood, and the beautiful young mother who died before Abby ever got the chance to know her. And there was her uncle, telling the whole world all about them.

"Are you out of your mind?" Abby yelled into the phone.

"Calm down, Abigail," Stan said.

"What gives you the right?" she demanded.

"They're going to find out about it all anyway," he reasoned. "I think it's best if they get it from us first. That way we control the spin."

"This is not a campaign, you asshole. My brother is on trial for his life."

"I am shocked, Abigail. I thought an experienced reporter like you would know better than that. Whether you're running for governor or on trial for murder, good press is good press. A well planned campaign can always turn the tide."

Abby slammed the phone down so hard it made her hand sting. She knew her uncle was right.

SIX

"WHAT?" ABBY GROWLed when she answered the phone at five-thirty the following morning.

"Mesmerizing interview with your uncle, love," Gordon said, sounding hurt. "Couldn't you have steered him in our direction?"

"I didn't know he was doing it," Abby said, rolling over.

"You're not privy to his public schedule?" Gordon asked.

"Not if I can help it."

"Well, if you won't speak to us, the least you can do is throw your family members that are willing to talk our way."

Abby told Gordon she'd see what she could do. She was hoping that would be the end of the conversation and she could go back to sleep, but Gordon kept talking.

"I also need some photographs of your brother. The only thing we have is his mug shot, love. Is that really the image of him you want people to see?"

She rubbed her eyes. She knew he had a point. "I don't know if I have anything here, I may have to get it from my dad's place."

"How is your father faring through all this?" Gordon asked.

"As well as can be expected," Abby said. She thought Gordon's inquiry actually sounded genuine.

"Good. You coming in today?"

"After the sun comes up."

"Great," Gordon said. "We need to talk, love. Bring the pictures with you."

LATER THAT MORNING, after she had showered, dressed and made coffee, Abby dug out a couple of shoeboxes from deep within her hall closet. They were filled with a couple of decade's worth of photographs she had never gotten around to organizing. She had to search through quite a few, but she did manage to find several photographs of Bennett. Most were from high school, but two were a bit more recent: one she had taken at the beach the summer before and one from a barbeque they had both attended a couple of years ago. Both showed Bennett happy and smiling. There were others but they all had Bennett either holding a drink or making a stupid face. Not exactly the images she wanted plastered on national TV.

"LISTEN LOVE," GORDON said. "There's no easy way to say this, so I'm just going to say it. I need you to take some time off."

"Excuse me?" Abby cocked her head towards her boss in order to hear him better. She was sitting on the couch in his office next to Sigmund, who was looking at the photographs of her brother she had just handed them.

"I need you to take some time off," Gordon repeated.

Abby was confused. "What do you mean time off?"

"I need you not to come to work for a while."

"What are you talking about?"

"A leave of absence," Sigmund translated.

Abby couldn't believe what she was hearing. "You have got to be kidding me."

"I'm afraid not," Gordon said, leaning back in his chair. "We need to get into this story, love, and we can't do it with you here."

"What about plague week?" she sputtered. "What about my stories?"

"Screw plague week, Abigail," Gordon said. "Emily Boyle's funeral is today! We're placing our sweeps schedule on the shitheap and going with this."

"Yeah," Abby muttered, "you and every other show on television."

"Can you really blame us?" Gordon asked. "Look beyond your personal involvement, love. This story is huge, and it's only getting started."

"Is that so? I didn't realize. I thought it only seemed big to me because I'm living it."

Gordon's tone softened. "Abigail, please. It's only temporary."

"I don't care whether it's temporary or tattooed on your fat ass, Gordon."

"Abigail," Sigmund chided. "We realize you're going through a rough patch right now."

"Up yours, Sigmund," Abby said.

"Be quiet, Sigmund," Gordon hissed. "Listen, I know that you are going through a horrendous time right now, and I will help you in any way possible, but the fact of the matter is I can't have you around here during this. It would appear improper. Our objectivity would be compromised,"

"Your *objectivity*?" Abby almost choked on the words. "Exactly what kind of objectivity is required to produce a three-part series on male breast implants? What about my sanity? I work my ass off for you people. Don't do this to me now. Please."

Gordon shifted uncomfortably in his seat. "Be reasonable, love. You've got to see my side here. I don't want to do this, but I can't jump into this bloody story properly with a major player sitting on my staff. You have my word that I will do whatever possible to help you and your family through this, but I can't have you in this office while this story is going on. It's nothing personal, it's only for a limited time and you'll still be paid."

Abby stood up. "Thanks for your support, guys. I guess it really is times like these when you find out who your true friends are."

"I am your friend," Gordon said.

"You sure have a funny way of showing it, Gordo," Abby said as she stormed out of his office.

ABBY COLLECTED her things as fast as possible and left. She didn't want to give anyone in the newsroom the satisfaction of watching her unravel. She bought two king sized snickers bars from a deli on Third Avenue and ate both as she walked back to her place. She was too upset to sit around her apartment alone, so she changed her clothes and headed out to see her brother.

"I am really sorry," Bennett said after she told him about her latest career turn. "This is all my fault."

"You're absolutely right, it is."

Bennett rubbed his eyes. "Maybe I should listen to Stan and Cates."

Abby didn't like the sound of that. "About what?"

"About taking the plea. They told me it would make things easier all around. I'm starting to think they may have the right idea."

"Easier?" Abby asked.

"On The Doctor, on you."

"On Stan's re-election."

"I suppose, but look what happened with your job. I don't even want to think about what this is doing to Dad."

"Don't worry about me," Abby assured him. "I'll be fine. And The Doctor is getting better all the time."

"They say if we go to trial and we lose, I could wind up in the electric chair."

"Connecticut doesn't use the electric chair anymore. They switched to lethal injection."

"Great," Bennett said. "That sounds much better."

"I don't even think your case qualifies. Besides, you didn't do this, remember?"

"They say it doesn't matter."

"Who are they?" Abby asked trying to keep her anger out of her voice.

"Cates."

Abby was dumbfounded. "Your defense attorney doesn't believe your innocence matters?"

"They brought a district attorney in to talk to me."

"They what?"

Bennett got up and walked over to the room's solitary window. He had to stand on his toes to see out of it. "Cates said if I plead to manslaughter I'll get ten years and be home in three. Considering the alternative, I don't think it sounds like such a bad deal."

"Bennett, please," she tried to reason with him. "You can't take the easy way out on this. I know you want this all to go away, and I know they're telling you that it's the best way, but it's not. We've got to fight this. I think our first step should be to seek alternate counsel."

"Fight this?" He shouted, turning around to face her. "I'm the one sitting in jail, not you."

"Bennett…"

"Abby, they're offering me three years, three goddamn years, if I plead. If I go to trial and lose, they might kill me."

"You didn't do this, but if you take the deal you might as well have."

"They said it would be easier for everyone involved." Bennett went back to trying to see out the window.

"Who's everyone? Who?" she yelled at her brother. "*You* are it, Bennett. You're the one who'd go to jail, you're the one who would be known forever as the animal who killed Emily Boyle and got away with it. Are you ready to tell the world that you beat her to death? You didn't do this."

"According to everyone but you that doesn't make a whole lot of difference."

"And what do you think?"

"I think I'm fucked."

"Besides that," Abby asked.

Bennett sunk into a chair. "I didn't lay a hand on her. I wouldn't do that."

"Then why do you want to say you did?"

Bennett didn't answer.

"Good," Abby said, standing up. "I think the first thing we do is tell Uncle Stan to get lost. Then we find another lawyer, one who is a bit more inclined to fight this thing. Then we can thank Boyd Cates for all of his help and concern and send him and his ugly shoes on their way."

"WELL, I THINK he should plead guilty," Boyd Cates told Abby.

"Well, I think you're full of crap."

"Abigail, please," Uncle Stan admonished her. "That really won't help matters."

After Abby left the jail she headed straight for her uncle's office. She was surprised to find Boyd Cates there, too.

"You know, Uncle Stan, my father's stroke is probably the best thing that could happen to you. If he was here he'd kill you."

Stan tried to reason with her. "Do you want to see this get worse? Do you know what a circus a trial would be?"

"Oh, geez, by all means let's avoid a messy trial. We'll just pack Bennett off to prison for the rest of his life. You're not even pretending to defend him!"

"That's utter nonsense," Cates exhaled.

"Have you gotten the autopsy report yet?" she asked.

"I am well aware of the autopsy results," Cates answered, sounding offended.

"But have you gotten the report?" she persisted.

"I don't really see the relevance," Cates said, looking at the congressman. "And I really don't appreciate the nature of this conversation."

But Abby wouldn't let up. She asked him if he thought Bennett leaving the apartment to get food around the time Emily died might warrant some further investigation.

"Ms. Gardner, you don't seem to realize that if your brother's case goes to trial, he could spend the rest of his life in prison or worse," Cates warned.

"And exactly what kind of sentence do you think he'd get if he takes the plea and tells the planet that he beat Emily Boyle to death?" Abby asked.

"Abby," Stan tried to interrupt.

"Do you think people would just forget about it? That when he's released from prison, if he gets through prison, that the world would simply say, 'oh yeah, he's paid his debt to society, let's let him live in peace and prosper?' His life would be over."

Cates disagreed. "If he takes the deal and pleads guilty, he'll be out in a few years. Do you really want him to take that kind of gamble? Do you want to be responsible for that? It will be on your head."

"But he didn't do anything," Abby reminded him.

"That doesn't really matter," Cates said.

"Stop saying that!" Abby yelled. "He didn't do anything!"

"Abigail, please," Stan implored her. "He'll listen to you. Tell him to take the plea. I've been promised he'll go away quickly for a few years and this will all die down."

"If he goes to trial you will be taking an enormous risk," Cates warned.

"We'll take our chances," Abby said. Then she stormed out of her second office of the day.

SEVEN

"WHAT ARE YOU going to do, love?" Maxwell Markham asked from atop his favorite barstool at The Ocean Club, "The Journal's" unofficial staff hangout. "Bounce back and forth between your brother in his jail cell and your father in his hospital bed and then tell them every week or so, 'oops, so sorry boys, some mass murderer in Omaha just farted and I have to dash out there for a couple of days to cover it? You two fellows take care of each other for the weekend.'"

"I didn't say I wanted to be out on the road," Abby said.

"Take care of your own first, love. The rest will work itself out."

Abby had found Maxwell M. Markham loitering outside of her apartment building when she arrived home that evening. She took him down to The Ocean Club because he seemed to be frightening her doorman. She had never invited Markham up to her apartment and didn't think now would be a good time to start. She had heard stories of people asking him in for only a moment and somehow winding up with him staying for a month.

At The Ocean Club, Markham had generously ordered a white wine for Abby and a bottle of tequila for himself. He put both on Gordon Burrows' tab.

"It's not fair," Abby said.

"I know it stings, Abigail," Markham said, emptying his glass. "But I truly believe it's in your best interest. You've got yourself a full plate at the moment and Gordon doesn't really have a choice. I've got to concur with him on this one. How is he supposed to go after this story at full throttle with you sitting there in on the story meetings?"

"There are other stories," Abby said. She wasn't in the mood to drink, so she just moved the glass around on the bar in front of her.

47

"At this precise moment in time, my dear, there is only one story, and you are sitting right on its nose."

"That's not my fault," she pointed out, hoping she didn't sound like she was pouting.

"Of course it's not," Markham said. "Hopefully this sordid tale will fade away promptly and you will back in the trenches forthwith."

"You don't honestly believe that, do you?"

"Not really. But please, I'm making a bid to be soothing, love."

"Great," she said, pushing her wine glass away.

Markham poured himself another drink. "You are aware that if there is anything I can do to be of assistance to you, you only need to ask."

"I need a lawyer," Abby told him.

"I thought you had already retained counsel?"

"Yeah, well, we're un-retaining Cates. We're thinking of going with a new legal strategy. We need to find someone who's actually interested in defending Bennett."

"Excellent," Markham said, banging his fist on the bar for emphasis. "I know precisely the chap."

"Who?" Abby asked.

"A superb barrister," Markham crowed.

"Who?"

"An effulgent litigator."

"Who?" Abby asked again, getting annoyed.

"Howard Eugene Smileowitz, Esquire."

Abby had heard of Smileowitz. "The mob lawyer?"

"He's not a mob lawyer, love, at least not exclusively. Besides, who do you think employs criminal defense attorneys, Girl Scouts?"

"I don't know, Markham. I just can't picture my brother and someone named Jimmy the Fish sharing legal counsel."

"Careful now Abigail, that white-Anglo upbringing of yours is showing again. The man is an absolutely inspired solicitor."

"I'll bet," Abby said.

"Plus he detests The Boyles."

"Why?"

Markham shrugged. "You'll have to ask him yourself."

EVERY PROGRAM ON television that evening led with Emily Boyle's funeral. Each showed virtually identical footage of the scores of mourners pouring into the church, as well as the hundreds more who stood outside and listened to the service on loudspeakers. Members of the press came close to outnumbering the mourners.

Emily was eulogized by family, friends and clergy alike as a beautiful young woman, loved and admired by many, whose life was cruelly cut short before she could make her mark on the world.

The Boyle-in-Charge appeared to be Thomas. Members of the press, who had been restrained behind police barricades, went wild after the service when he led the mourners out of the church, gently grasping the elbow of his only surviving sibling, Cassandra.

Not a lot was known about the youngest of Gilbert Boyle's children. Her brother Thomas regularly sought out the press, and her sister Emily, whether she wanted to or not, often seemed to make headlines, but Cassandra Boyle was different. She kept a very low profile, was rarely photographed at charity functions or society parties, and was never spotted leaving a chic club at three o'clock in the morning on the arm of some known felon or famous actor. She kept company with a tight circle of friends who observed one ground rule: never, ever talk to the press.

IMMEDIATELY AFTER THE service, Gwen Mason stopped to read a statement to the press. She was the only one who did.

"This was one of the saddest days of my life," Gwen said, wiping away her tears from behind her sunglasses. "It's almost too sad for me to talk about. Today we buried my good friend, and I am grief-stricken and angry because of it. I cannot believe that Emily is gone, and I honestly don't know what I will do without her. It's just so unfair, so, so unfair."

Abby had dealt with people like Gwen Mason before: friends of the victim who liked seeing themselves on TV. She knew that eventually the media and the public would grow bored with her, possibly even turn on her. The difficult part was going to be to try and ignore her in the meantime.

Thomas Boyle's press conference was a bit more reserved. He met with reporters at the family attorney's office later that afternoon. Not surprisingly, Cassandra Boyle was nowhere to be seen. She had vanished once again.

"On behalf of my family, I would like to extend our deepest gratitude to the people of this great nation, as well as the world, who have mourned along with us at the senseless loss of my sister, Emily. We take great comfort in your thoughts and prayers. Emily's life may have been short, but it was not without meaning. Her kindness and her zeal for life touched many people during her brief stay on this earth, and I, for one, take comfort in the knowledge that she is now in a better place, safe in heaven with my parents and my brother, Gilbert."

Thomas paused to push an errant lock of hair off of his forehead. "I also want to thank the many members of the law enforcement community who worked so quickly and tirelessly to apprehend a suspect in Emily's murder. We know that justice will be swift and fair in its treatment of this disturbed young man, and hope to see him prosecuted to the fullest extent of the law."

EIGHT

"WHAT DO YOU know about Thomas Boyle?" Abby asked as she watched her brother walk the perimeter of the jail's visitor's room.

"You mean besides that he's a complete tool?" Bennett asked.

"Did you spend a lot of time with him?"

"Fortunately, no," Bennett said. "He and Emily didn't exactly get along."

Abby noticed her brother's voice still cracked whenever he said Emily's name.

He told her that Emily barely spoke to Thomas. "She thought he was a pretentious, narcissistic prick. He loved all that 'American Royalty' crap–all the attention, the heads turning, the common folk whispering--she couldn't stand it."

"What did he and Emily fight about?"

"Usually each other's existence. She was nauseated by his whole social climbing, boy wonder of politics, holier than thou crap."

"And he?"

"He thought his sister was a career liability for him and he made the mistake of thinking she would give a shit."

"Liability?" Abby asked.

"The drugs, the boyfriends, it all embarrassed him. He thought the whole bad-girl thing would hurt his career. Like anyone would care. He had this wholesome, toothy, Boyle family image in his head. The same garbage most of the country believes and Emily just wasn't going along with it to his satisfaction."

Bennett told Abby that Cassandra Boyle didn't get along too well with Thomas, either.

"Were she and Emily close?" Abby asked.

"They didn't see each other a lot, but they'd talk on the phone. The Boyles and The Lelands own a lot of homes, and Emily said Cassandra had keys to all of them. She'd spend a couple of weeks in New York, then Newport, then Hilton Head, then she'd go to Europe for a couple of months."

"Sounds like a rough life," Abby said.

"I only met her a couple of times. We got along okay, but she didn't strike me as an overly happy person."

"Why?"

Bennett shrugged. "She just didn't. I think she had a real hard time with the whole 'Boyle' thing. She wanted even less to do with it than Emily."

"So, I guess she didn't do much campaign work for Thomas."

"No," Bennett laughed. "She and Emily kept their distance from big brother and his political aspirations."

"Yeah, well, between big brother's political aspirations and Gwen whatever-her-name-is, we're getting killed out there."

"Gwen Mason?" Bennett asked.

"She seems real fond of you."

"She hates my guts."

"Any reason in particular?"

"Gwen knew I told Emily that I didn't think they should be hanging out together. Gwen's a total coke head and Emily didn't need to be around that."

ABBY WAS STUNNED by Howard Smileowitz's offices. She had never seen so much black Formica before in her life.

After her daily visits with her brother and her father, Howard Smileowitz made for an interesting change of pace. The mob lawyer-friend of Markham's looked exactly as Abby had imagined-- short, fat and tan–with an unlit cigar resting in the corner of his mouth. The attorney wore an expensive-looking gray pinstriped suit which happened to coordinate nicely with his office furniture. His thinning hair was slicked back on the sides and gathered tightly in a well-gelled ponytail that Abby thought resembled the squiggly appendage one would find on the posterior of a pig. She had an incredible urge to pull it but restrained herself.

Smileowitz sported a gold tie bar; something that normally would distress Abby, as she was raised to hold very strong beliefs regarding men's neckwear jewelry. But on Howard Smileowitz, it seemed to work. He wore a school ring on his left hand and a big diamond pinkie ring on his right. His wrists were heavy with precious metals as well. An enormous gold watch encircled the left one; on the right was a thick gold-link bracelet that Abby was sure was heavy enough to secure an ocean liner to a pier.

"From what I can tell what they've got against your brother ain't exactly rock solid," Smileowitz told Abby as they sat in his office. "The evidence against him is circumstantial, and your brother claims to have been out picking up some food for thirty minutes before he found her unconscious. In a murder defense, thirty minutes is an eternity."

Abby liked what she was hearing.

"Then there's the whole press thing. The attention has been fucking unbelievable, if you will excuse my French. But it can work for him. It raises a lot of questions about his ability to get a fair trial. Unfortunately, at the same time, you've got a D.A. who, because of all the publicity, is under a lot of pressure, and that's not good. Overzealous and prosecutor," he said, shaking his head, "never a good combo."

Smileowitz told Abby he wanted to take a look at some things and talk to a few people before he'd commit to the case. He promised he'd call the next day.

As Smileowitz walked her out, Abby asked him why he hated the Boyles so much.

Smileowitz laughed. "I don't hate all of them, just that prick, Thomas."

"I keep hearing that word associated with him," Abby said.

"Trust me. It fits the little shit."

"What do you have against him?"

"If I decide to take the case I'll enlighten you. Rest assured: my personal feelings would only work in your brother's favor."

"I always respect a good grudge."

"Good," Smileowitz laughed. "I'll be in touch."

THE NEWS PROGRAMS on the day after the funeral didn't have anything fresh to tell the viewing public about the case, so they rehashed what everyone already knew and trotted out Gwen Mason again.

Emily's purported best friend was interviewed about a lucrative book contract she had just signed: for an undisclosed amount of money, she was going to tell the general public everything that they ever wanted to know about her beloved friend Emily Boyle.

"As an added bonus," she promised, "the book is also going to include sixteen pages of never-before seen color photographs of Em from my personal collection."

Abby was surprised it had taken Gwen as long as it did to sign a book deal. She had already heard a reporter from the *New York Journal* got a contract to pen a quick, straight-to-paperback about Emily Boyle's murder. She knew within six to eight months of publication both tomes would devolve into TV movies.

She refused to watch "The Journal" on principal, so instead she flipped between the competition. "The Beat" featured an interview with Ted Walton, who Abby thought looked vaguely familiar. He told the reporter he and Bennett had been friends as kids, and that he recalled Bennett being suspended from their middle school several times for smoking, cutting classes and using a cherry bomb to blow up a toilet. "Late Edition" was taking its viewers on what they promised was an exclusive tour of several of the preparatory schools and colleges that Bennett had been expelled from. "The Report" had them scooped, though. They must have either bought, or sneaked their way into, another condominium in the luxurious complex where Emily Boyle had lived. They claimed it had an identical floor plan to the one where Emily Boyle had spent her final moments on this earth. They did a fascinating four-and-a-half minute piece on a walk through of an empty three-bedroom duplex with an eat-in kitchen, fireplace and two-and-a-half baths.

THE PHONE AT ABBY'S bedside rang at five a.m.

"What?" Abby grumbled into the phone.

"Ms. Gardner, Howard Smileowitz here. I've done some nosing around. I think we can work something out."

Abby was suddenly wide awake. "Good."

"We need to talk. Can you meet me at my office at eleven-thirty?"

"I'll be there," she promised.

"I'll need you to bring along a retainer."

"How much do you want?"

"Seventy-five grand to start."

Abby felt her tongue begin to swell. "I assume you'll take a check."

"From you?" Smileowitz laughed. "Not a problem."

"YOU HIRED WHAT?" Bennett asked as he stubbed his cigarette out on the floor of the visitor's room.

"Don't start," Abby said.

"I'm going to be defended by a consigliore?"

"Look," she told him, "Boyd Cates might be a partner in the whitest, white shoe firm in our solar system, but he was making reservations for you in maximum security. Howard Smileowitz has actually expressed an interest in defending you."

"Yes, me, and Fat Paulie, and Sammy Bones, and Tony the Bull..."

"I never knew you to be so small-minded," Abby said, cutting him off.

"Yeah, well, this place brings out the very finest in all who pass through its urine-stained halls."

"Smileowitz is supposed to be the best."

"Well, I certainly hope you wouldn't retain a mediocre mafia attorney to defend me."

"You are going to have to trust me on this."

Bennett leaned back in his chair. "Do I have a choice?"

"Not really," Abby said.

"Well then, in that case, I trust you completely."

"THE FIRST THING I do is I meet with your brother. Alone," Howard Smileowitz explained. "There are some things he might not want to tell me with his little sister around."

"Okay," Abby agreed. She couldn't imagine what her brother would be reluctant to discuss in her presence. "But you do understand that I want to be involved in this."

"Are you a lawyer?" Smileowitz asked, pointing his cigar at Abby.

"No."

"Are you a defendant?"

"No." Abby could sense where this was headed.

"Then I am confused as to what exactly your role in this defense would be?"

"You mean besides writing you large checks?"

Smileowitz laughed. "Precisely."

Abby reminded him that she was an experienced investigative journalist who at the moment had a lot of time on her hands.

"And you want to do some snooping around?" Smileowitz asked.

"Exactly."

"Let me talk to this brother of yours. Then I'll cash this check. Then I'll see what we can do." Smileowitz stood up, ready to walk Abby to the door, but she remained seated.

"What do you have against Thomas Boyle?" she asked. "You told me if you took the case you'd tell me."

"The guy is a prick."

"That much I know, I was hoping for some new information."

Smileowitz shook his head. "Little Lord Fauntleroy was an assistant D.A. in Brooklyn, maybe ten years ago. His first case was against a client of mine, Eddie 'The Tooth' Briscoe."

"The Tooth?" Abby asked.

"Yeah, dental hygiene wasn't his strong suit," Smileowitz said. "It was a simple assault and battery. And the press, who would cover Boyle's bowel movements if he'd let them, were, of course, all over it. Tommy-boy thought it was a slam dunk, but I rammed it right down his throat."

Smileowitz explained that Thomas' work was sloppy and The Tooth walked. "Boyle could also never seem to make it back from the lunch break on time, something which was my great pleasure to point out to the judge on more than one occasion. The judge called him out about it in front of the admiring media. Threatened to hold him in contempt. The little shit was livid."

"That would explain why he hates you," Abby said.

"It gets worse. A few years back, my kid sister Rita is up for a job at the Justice Department. She's brilliant--Harvard Law Review, top of her class, a legal genius. All she wants to do is prosecute bad guys. Thomas figures this is the way to get back at me. He puts the word out and suddenly the Justice Department wants nothing to do with her. The district attorneys don't want to come near her, either. Her prosecutorial career was finished before it ever began. The asshole couldn't beat me so he picks on my little sister."

"What's she doing now?" Abby asked.

"Rita? She's the top litigator at Bloom, Steier and Manley, makes about four hundred large a year before bonuses. Youngest person to make partner in the history of the firm."

"Not bad," Abby said.

"She does okay," Smileowitz said smoothing his ponytail. "But she really wanted to chase bad guys."

After meeting with Smileowitz, Abby went to see her father. Surprisingly, telling The Doctor about the change of counsel went smoothly. Abby was concerned about her father's reaction to switching Bennett's defense from a Park Avenue law firm to a man whose clients usually paid him with attaché cases full of small, non-sequentially numbered tens and twenties.

"I'm confident in your judgment on these matters, Abigail," The Doctor said, his speech improving with each syllable. "You haven't disappointed me yet."

Abby narrowed her gaze at her father. "Who are you?"

The Doctor laughed. He didn't realize Abby wasn't kidding. Father and daughter spent a surprisingly pleasant couple of hours together working on the *Times* crossword puzzle and discussing Bennett's case. Shortly before her father was to go into his afternoon therapy session, Abby's cell phone rang.

"Abigail, love," Gordon Burrows bellowed into the phone. "So glad I found you."

"What do you want?" she asked, annoyed at the sound of his voice.

"Did you see Gwen Mason in *Us* magazine?"

"No."

"Definitely worth checking out. I didn't bother reading what they wrote about her, but her pictures were taken poolside wearing a thong. A little ambitious on Ms. Mason's part, if you ask me."

"Is that why you're calling?"

"No, actually, I wanted to give you a heads up about "American Magazine" tonight. Apparently, they have some sort of bombshell on the Emily Boyle story that they are planning on launching into orbit this evening."

"Any idea what it is?"

"No, but if I find out anything else, I'll call. I heard you switched mouthpieces. Excellent move. Smileowitz is a brilliant son of a bitch, absolutely the best."

THE SELF-IMPORTANT TELEVISION journalists who bring "American Magazine" to the viewing public each week usually prided themselves on staying out of the fray when it came to the ordinary sordid murder and mayhem tales that the rest of the industry spent most of their time chasing. The death of Emily Boyle, however, was far from an ordinary murder.

Nothing made this fact more apparent than when Joely Rogan and the folks at "American Magazine" did a half-gainer straight into the middle of the story.

Raven-haired, beautiful, and desperately serious, Joely Rogan was the highest paid female journalist in the country. A former White House correspondent and Miss Teenage Rhode Island, she rose through the network ranks at lightening speed to anchor the top-rated news magazine program in the country. And she reinforced her status as the biggest of the best that night when she introduced the world to a handsome young man named Campbell Dawson.

Dawson, in turn, cemented his place in the psyche of the media-viewing world with just five little words.

"Emily Boyle," he said, "was my fiancée."

Sitting on her couch, watching Joely Rogan help build her brother's motive for murdering Emily Boyle, Abby's brain started to ache.

"We met about four months ago at a party," Dawson confessed between sniffles. "I was aware she was seeing Bennett Gardner at the time, but it didn't matter. It was love at first sight."

Dawson appeared to be in his late thirties. A handsome, blonde investment consultant, he looked like the type whose tennis game was only exceeded by his yachting skills.

"We were together as often as we could manage, stolen evenings, weekends. We went to London last month, and she promised me she would break it off with Gardner. Unfortunately, right after we returned, his father suffered a stroke and that delayed things. Emily told me that Gardner was normally off balance, even somewhat disturbed, and that sometimes she was afraid of him. His father's illness made him even more emotional."

"When did you propose to her?" Joely asked.

"About three weeks ago. I asked her to marry me and she accepted. It was the happiest three weeks of my life, and I think hers as well. I gave her a ring, but she asked me to hold on to it until she could break things off completely with Gardner. The last time I spoke to her she promised me she was going to end it that evening. She told me his father was doing better and she felt now was the time. She said she loved me before she hung up the phone. I never spoke to her again." Dawson's voice cracked with emotion.

Abby couldn't even begin to estimate the effect Campbell Dawson's revelations, whether true or not, would have on her brother's case. The media was going to suck this up like a thick chocolate milkshake.

She was glad Smileowitz had cashed her check that morning.

NINE

"I SUPPOSE YOU didn't know anything about that Joely Rogan garbage when you came to see me yesterday?" Smileowitz asked during his second consecutive five A.M. phone call to Abby.

Abby cradled the phone between her head and her pillow. "Don't you ever sleep?"

"When I need sleep, I sleep."

It wasn't too early in the morning for Abby to fully appreciate the irony of the situation. For the first time in years, she knew that Gordon Burrows wouldn't be calling her before sunrise. And, instead, someone else had swept in to take his place.

"You ever heard of this Dawson putz before?"

"Not until last night."

"Well, between Gwen Mason and this idiot, the viewing public is getting an earful, and none of it is working in our favor. We need to have a serious talk with your brother today; kick his ass a bit, you know, make sure he's telling us everything. I don't like surprises."

"Really? I don't like five A.M. phone calls."

"Tough," Smileowitz laughed. "You said you wanted to be a part of this."

"DID YOU KNOW about him?" Abby asked her brother.

"What do you mean?" Bennett asked.

"I think it's a pretty simple question," Howard Smileowitz said as he paced the length of the jail visitors' room. "Did you know about this Dawson guy before yesterday?"

"Sort of," Bennett said with a shrug.

"Sort of," Smileowitz repeated. "What is this bullshit? Either you did or you didn't."

"Sometimes she saw other guys. I imagine this Dawson person was one of them."

"You're very understanding," Smileowitz said.

"We had an open relationship."

"Does that mean you saw other people, too?" Abby asked.

"No, that was more Emily's thing."

Smileowitz stopped pacing. "You must be the world's most understanding boyfriend."

"I loved her."

"This jerk-off said she was going to marry him," Smileowitz said.

"I highly doubt it."

"Why?" Abby asked.

"Emily was going to marry every man she ever met. This Dawson guy just hadn't figured that out yet."

"And you had it all figured out?" Smileowitz asked.

"As a matter of fact, I did," Bennett said, crossing his arms across his chest. "I knew Emily and I wouldn't be together forever, but that didn't bother me. I've never really been one to concern myself all that much with the future."

"YOUR BROTHER IS A strange man," Smileowitz told Abby as they walked out to their cars.

"I realize that."

"Strange doesn't always play well with juries," he warned.

"I know. Bennett's got a lot of problems," Abby said as they approached her car, "but he's a good person. You just have to get to know him."

"I plan to. I've got a couple of my investigators nosing around, looking into exactly what your brother was up to the night Emily Boyle died. They're also checking out some of Emily's lesser-known associates."

"You mean the ones Grandmother Boyle wouldn't have invited for Thanksgiving?"

"Precisely. Emily seems to have kept company with a number of people involved with supplying and indulging in various pharmaceutical habits."

"What about Gwen Mason?" Abby asked opening her car door and tossing her bag on the seat.

"Don't worry, I'm checking into her as well. It's all part of my job. Your job is going to be to get to know the Boyles better."

"Why?"

"You said you wanted to be a part of this. My guys are already working on the evidence and Gwen Mason, and now they'll get started on the boyfriends. I want you to find out everything you can about Emily and her family."

"Why?" Abby asked.

"Jesus Christ, is that how you answer every question?"

Abby smiled. "Most of the time."

"Why? Because we may want to try and counter the way Emily Boyle and her family are being portrayed. Remember, the key words here are 'reasonable doubt.'"

"You want me to dig up dirt on a dead woman and her family?"

"Yeah," Smileowitz smiled. "It will be like you're still working for 'The Journal.'"

TEN

Abby unlocked her two deadbolts and raced into her apartment to grab the ringing phone. "Hello?" she said gasping for breath.

"Abigail, love, is that you?"

She needn't have rushed, it was Markham. "Who do you think it is?" she asked.

"You sound terribly alluring when you're panting. Do you mind if I ask if you are perspiring?"

"What do you want?"

"Have you seen this week's *Weekly Globe*?"

The *Weekly Globe* was on the low end of the supermarket tabloid spectrum. Its journalistic exploits made the *Star* look like the *Washington Post*.

"No, I haven't," Abby said, thumbing through the mail she had picked up in the lobby. "Ill advisedly, I let my subscription lapse."

"Well, I'm certain you'll find this week's edition rather absorbing."

"I'm sure," Abby said, rolling her eyes. "What do they have? Emily Boyle was a space alien?"

"Not quite, love."

"Then what?"

"Are you in close proximity to anything breakable?"

"Why? What do they have?"

"Pictures of your father."

Abby ran to three different supermarkets before she located a *Weekly Globe*. It was on a rack next to the express lane in a Sloan's on Third Avenue. Right above the one-inch block print blaring *Ancient*

Skull Sings and Dances! were five words that made her heart drop right into her abdomen: *Emily's Accused Killer's Crippled Dad!*

Abby purchased a couple of copies of the *Globe* without making eye contact with the cashier. She didn't dare look at the pictures while in the store out of fear of what her reaction might be. Instead, she ran back to her apartment where she could examine them in private.

The captions on the three-page pictorial concluded that Bennett's arrest caused his father's stroke. The *Weekly Globe's* editorial department didn't seem to be too concerned with the actual chronology of the two events. The photographs were cruel; obviously taken through doorways or windows with a telephoto lens. The pictures emphasized The Doctor's physical weaknesses. They showed him trying to feed himself, trying to dress himself, trying to walk and while he was sleeping. The close-ups were the most brutal of all; in those pictures she thought her father looked like a pathetic, helpless old man. And the idea of tens of thousands of devoted *Globe* readers pouring over them made her stomach twist.

Abby called Markham, but all she got was his voice mail.

"You've got to find out who did this," Abby told him after the beep. "You've got to get me a name."

Then she headed for Harborview General.

"I WOULD BE truly interested in hearing your explanation for this," Abby said as she slammed the *Weekly Globe* onto the desk of Peter Renay, MD. "I'm confused as to exactly what the therapeutic benefits of something like this might be."

Dr. Renay's eyes widened as he read; a sign Abby took with great dismay to mean he had nothing to do with her father's debut in the national media.

"This is horrible, just horrible," he said, shaking his head.

"I thought so, too. Needless to say, my father will be completing his treatment elsewhere."

"Now, Ms. Gardner, I really don't think that's necessary."

"I'm sure you don't. But I'd like to prevent any follow-up stories that your staff might be working on."

"I can assure you..." he began.

"No, I don't think you can. I think you assured me several weeks ago that my father was being cared for in the finest facility around. At the time I didn't realize it included a press office."

BLOOD RELATIONS

Dr. Renay bristled at the accusation. "You don't know that these photographs originated with a member of my staff."

"Who the hell do you think arranged for them, my father?"

"Now see here..."

"No, you see here, Doctor. Believe me, I will find out who did this. And when I do, his ass, as well as yours, will be mine."

ABBY SPOKE WITH Bennett, Smileowitz and her father's physicians. All thought the best possible thing for The Doctor's recovery and safety would be for him to be cared for in his own home. Abby thought it was an easy solution for them to come up with since none of them would be the one responsible for actually caring for him.

ABBY SPENT THAT night in her beloved apartment knowing that it would probably be her last for the foreseeable future. There was only one bright spot to her evening. It came in the form of a story "The Report" aired. It was yet another sit-down interview with Gwen Mason.

The interview rehashed everything Gwen had been saying to the press about Bennett, Emily, and herself--the last subject being the most interesting part. Somehow, reporter Craig London convinced Gwen to take a look at a videotape that he had brought along with him. After a few seconds of watching the tape, she became quite irate. This was perfectly understandable considering the tape featured somewhat amateurish, but perfectly clear, footage of her performing oral sex on a man identified as her former husband's brother. The graphic video had been provided by Gwen Mason's former sister-in-law, who was also kind enough to inform the show of Gwen's history of alcohol and drug abuse, which had culminated in her arrest for drug possession eight months before.

"You son of a bitch! Get out of my house!" Gwen yelled as she lunged for the camera.

Most of the rest of her interview had to be bleeped because of F.C.C. regulations. It didn't matter. Even without sound, the footage the cameraperson continued to shoot as they were being tossed out of her house conveyed the mood and tone perfectly.

"The drug charges were dropped," Gwen Mason's former sister-in-law explained in a separate interview. "Because her father is a very rich man. Sometimes, that's all it takes."

The story ended with footage of London again trying to elicit a response from the suddenly camera-shy Gwen as she helped throw him and his crew out of her house. Between the obscenities that had to be bleeped out, Gwen could be heard telling him, uncharacteristically, that she had nothing more to say.

ABBY QUESTIONED SMILEOWITZ about Gwen Mason's alleged arrest when he called her at six o'clock the following morning.

"It ain't alleged. And from what my sources tell me, she was originally charged with dealing, not possession."

"I knew something wasn't right about her. We need to find out who she was dealing to, where she was getting it..."

"Whoa, step back a second. *We* don't have to do anything. I do, and I've got Gwen Mason covered. My guys are all over this."

"But...

"No buts, Gardner. If you really want to help your brother just stay away and let me do my job."

LATER THAT MORNING, Dr. Renay revised his original position regarding Abby's plans to remove her father from his care. This change of heart occurred immediately following his arrival at work where he found fifteen reporters waiting to speak with him. By the time he got to his office, he couldn't do enough to help send The Doctor home.

Abby couldn't bring herself to show her father the pictures in the *Weekly Globe*. She simply told him the press had found out about him and everyone agreed it would be in the best interest of his continued progress and safety if he proceeded with his rehabilitative therapy at home. The Doctor was beyond thrilled.

With the help of Helen, The Doctor's longtime nurse, Abby was able to secure all of the equipment necessary to convert the downstairs den in her father's house into a quasi-hospital room. Dr. Renay did his share by arranging for visiting physical, speech and occupational therapists as well as nursing care. Hudson, the physical therapist, would be responsible for The Doctor's therapy by day. His nursing and nutritional needs would be the domain of a beefy Bavarian woman named Olga, and Helen promised to come by in the afternoons to help out as well. Abby's duties would operate on a twenty-four hour basis and be far less defined.

Miraculously, Abby had only one minor disagreement with her father regarding his return home. It concerned his Labrador retriever, Maggie, who had been in Helen's care since The Doctor's stroke. Abby had never lived in the house with the dog, and she didn't think the present would be the best time to start. It wasn't that Abby didn't like animals--she did. The problem was that Maggie hated Abby. She figured that the dog sensed the tension Abby felt every time she was in her father's house and resented it. She manifested this resentment by growling at Abby, trying to physically restrict her movement around the house, and general all around snotty-ness. Abby tried to persuade her father that having Maggie constantly underfoot in the house might be dangerous and it would be best if she remained with Helen for the time-being. But The Doctor didn't buy it. Both Maggie and Abby would be moving back home.

THE FAMILIAR ODOR of her childhood hit Abby as soon as she walked into the house. The blend of sea air and wood polish permeated every inch of the place. She breathed it in as she carried her bags up the stairs to her room and placed them neatly on her bed. Her father's house was spotless. Always had been. Dust barely had a chance to settle before it was chased away by The Doctor or his housekeeper. Abby didn't remember her mother, but had been told throughout her life about her flawless cleaning skills.

Adele Seaton was a registered nurse. She had met Abby's father while he was still an intern. A couple of years older than The Doctor and Jewish, she wasn't exactly the spouse his social-register family had in mind. She was thirty-nine when she died.

After the death of his wife, The Doctor raised Abby and Bennett alone. He never remarried, and as far as Abby knew, he never even had a date.

With her brother away at school, and The Doctor spending most of his time at work, Abby was often alone in the house. Each day after school, she would check in at her father's office, and then go home. On most days before heading into the house Abby would take a detour by the beach. Once inside, though, she would dutifully complete her homework, and then usually immerse herself in a steady stream of television, interrupted only by dinner with her father if he wasn't working late, until she went to bed.

She wasn't always left on her own. Two or three days a week the housekeeper would be there, and a couple of times a year her Uncle Stanley would come by and take her to dinner. Abby did have a few friends that she saw outside of school, but the truth was, like her father, Abby was happiest by herself. She had very little patience for other people.

Abby knew her first night back in her father's house would be strange, but she was hoping it would at least be uneventful. She and Maggie came to a preliminary understanding. They would ignore each other's presence and everything would be fine as long as Abby stayed out of the way and didn't make any sudden moves.

The Doctor was thrilled to be home. He had been beaming with the side of his face that worked ever since Abby told him she was taking him back to his house. Her father's smile was still something Abby had to get used to. It was as if he had suddenly grown mutton chop sideburns or a third ear. He was thrilled to see Maggie and began referring to his daughter and his dog as "his girls," a designation neither Abby nor Maggie seemed particularly pleased with.

On their first night home, father, daughter and large Labrador retriever all dined together in The Doctor's new room. The conversation was pleasant and the show tunes plentiful. Abby's father even spoke with his mouth full. It was quite a contrast to the dinners she remembered growing up--serious occasions filled with talk of current events, grades and very high expectations.

Abby watched television with her father until he fell asleep; then she retired to her room. Maggie followed Abby upstairs. She could hear the dog breathing as she slept outside her bedroom door. She figured Maggie felt she could serve her master better by knowing exactly where the enemy was at all times. Abby spent the rest of her premiere night back at Chez Gardner barricaded within her childhood room by ninety-five pounds of hostile Labrador retriever.

Except for a coat or two of white paint, the room hadn't changed one iota since she had moved out over a decade before. It still had all the warmth and personality of a Dickensonian orphanage. The sturdy, single oak bed, dresser and desk were exactly the way she'd left them. Growing up, Abby wasn't permitted to hang anything on the walls of her room. The Doctor didn't want tacks or tape marking the paint. The only adornment he allowed was a couple of shelves that were still filled with books from her childhood.

It was probably a good thing Abby couldn't sleep that night. If she had been able to drift off she wouldn't have heard the window shattering downstairs. She cursed her father for refusing to jump into the twentieth century and install an alarm. She used her cell phone to dial 911 and then hit the floor with a bone-fracturing thud as she tripped over Maggie while attempting to race out of her room. The dog was so busy protecting The Doctor from his daughter that she apparently didn't have time to deal with whoever was breaking and entering downstairs. Abby pulled herself up, cursed the dog, and then began searching the upstairs for a weapon. All she found were antiques. What the Gardners lacked in defensive objects they certainly made up for in original mission furniture and late nineteenth century art. She was trying to figure out which valuable heirloom would make the best blunt object and still be covered by insurance when she heard a loud thud and someone yelling in German. Abby grabbed a porcelain water pitcher and raced downstairs with Maggie barking at her heels. There she found Olga standing over a young man lying motionless on the floor. In his hands was a camera, in hers, a much more effective frying pan.

Sirens wailed in the distance.

ELEVEN

"I DON'T KNOW what's gotten into these youngsters today. They're all—'Oh, look at me, I've got a bloody camera, I'm a journalist!'--No training, no experience, no pride in their work. What kind of a cretin breaks into a house without checking first to see if someone is home?" Markham shook his head in disgust. "Nobody wants to do the necessary research anymore."

The Sussex County Police were the first to arrive on the scene, followed in short order by Smileowitz and then Markham. Within half an hour, four more news crews and assorted print and radio reporters had joined the members of the press who were permanently stationed outside of the Gardners' house.

The Doctor woke up after the police arrived and demanded to know what was going on. Abby explained to him what had happened and assured him she had everything under control. She asked him to please go back to sleep and, much to her amazement, he did.

The photographer, who regained consciousness moments before the police arrived, wisely opted not to move any part of his body until Olga and her fryer were relieved of guard duty by several police officers. He told the police he was doing some freelance work for one of the British tabloids.

"Amateur," Markham spat. He was appalled when he found out the man had named his employer.

Smileowitz was disgusted as well. "First thing tomorrow I arrange for round-the-clock security, I apologize, I should have thought of it before."

Markham seconded the idea, but Abby declined the offer. "I don't think I need a rent-a-cop out here on an all night coffee and doughnut binge. As long as Olga has her kitchenware, we'll all be safe."

Smileowitz shook his head. "I'd feel better with some of my guys keeping an eye on the place. You won't even know that they're here."

Abby didn't want to imagine what *my guys* could entail. "I think we can manage on our own."

Markham put an arm around Abby's shoulder. "Listen love, Howard here tells me that you're going to be running out and about doing some investigating on the case at hand. Wouldn't you feel better knowing someone is here keeping an ocular cavity focused in your father's direction while you're not en locale?"

"Fine," Abby said realizing he had a point. "Just none of those old guys they have watching the parking lot at the high school, please."

"Only the best," Smileowitz assured her. "You won't even know they're around."

ABBY WAS EXHAUSTED the next morning as she used her laptop to surf the internet for information on the Boyles. Olga had awakened her at six-thirty. Her father had requested Abby's company at the breakfast table. She could tell that this togetherness-meal thing had the potential to really get out of hand.

The search engine she was using found close to ninety-thousand documents on the family. She started reading through them, but after the first ten hits the information got repetitive. Abby decided an afternoon visit to the library might provide some additional material.

EASTON'S DOWNTOWN HADN'T changed much since Abby was a small child. She parked in front of the Easton Public Library which was still located on Route 1A, next door to the Easton Volunteer Fire Department, and across the street from the Easton Diner. On the next block was the town's only gas station, which also was home to a truncated donut shop franchise. Next to the gas station was the hardware store, the liquor store and the butcher shop. One of the few things Abby thought her hometown had going for it was that it was too small for any of the major fast-food joints or chain stores to take an interest. The only new addition to the commercial district was a coffee house named appropriately enough, 'The Coffee House.' Abby had her doubts about the place, but was pleasantly surprised by the tall cup of the house blend she purchased before heading into the library.

The library had numerous tomes on the history of the Boyle clan that told the story of the family from the nineteenth century up through present time. The books ran the gamut from a thick volume tracing Wilson Banion Boyle's epic struggle to build a railroad empire while reinventing serfdom, to gleaming biographies of Gilbert Boyle Jr. and trashy paperback tell-alls on the third generation of Boyles running wild through high society and the Ivy League.

When Abby arrived home that evening she found a large box from "The Journal" waiting for her. The note inside was from Gordon.

Markham tells me you're doing some investigating on your brother's case. I thought this material might be of some assistance. Let me know if I can help with anything else.

The box contained copies of every story "The Journal's" tape librarians could dig up on the Boyles. It also included all the research materials they could pull from their files, plus anything they could glean from anyone else's.

Abby's quiet evening reading was disrupted by a phone call from Markham informing her that Campbell Dawson would be making another appearance on prime time television that night. This time on "The World This Evening."

"I understand our tragic Mr. Dawson will be discussing the wedding plans that were never meant to be," Markham told her.

Abby rubbed her tired eyes. "This guy has some press agent."

"Speaking of agents, I've heard some book deal rumors swirling about Dawson."

Abby wasn't surprised. "Everyone else is writing one, why shouldn't he?"

The interview went over the basics once again, just in case anyone in the viewing audience had recently been released from a sealed cave and had missed them. Then Dawson talked about the future he and Emily Boyle had planned together.

Something about this guy just didn't sit right with Abby, and it wasn't the fact that he was giving the world more reasons to think her brother guilty of murder. There was something about Campbell Dawson's smooth manner and always-appropriate answers that led Abby to believe that he wasn't exactly what he seemed to be.

Abby read about the Boyles until she fell asleep that night. Then she dreamt about them. In the morning she could recall only the one that had her manning the dessert table at Gilbert Boyle's wedding wearing nothing but a teddy, panties and a gas mask. As she served wedding cake, someone was whispering to her in German-tinged English.

"Miss Gardner, Miss Gardner."

Abby opened her eyes and was momentarily terrified by the sight of Olga leaning over her bed.

"Oh good, you are awake. Your father vish-es to see you."

"What's wrong?" Abby asked, jumping out of bed.

"He did not make that clear to me. He simply asked me to fetch you. He said he needed to speak vith you immediately."

Abby pulled on her robe as she raced down the stairs with Maggie in hot pursuit. The tee-shirt and boxer shorts she slept in kept her warm and were unrevealing, but definitely did not cover enough of her for the likes of her father. If he didn't think he might strangle himself, Charles Gardner would wear a necktie to sleep.

"What's wrong?" Abby said as she rushed to her father's side. The lights were on in his room and he was sitting up in bed.

"Abigail, we must talk. I need your help."

"What's the matter?"

"It's the tomatoes."

Abby wasn't sure what was going on. "The tomatoes?"

"Yes, yes, the tomatoes. And the cucumbers, as well."

"The cucumbers?" Abby repeated.

"The time is fast approaching. It is too late for seeds, but you must go to the nursery on Route 114. They'll help us. We'll make a list. Do you have a pen?"

Abby looked at the clock. "It's two o'clock in the morning."

"I'm well aware of the time, young lady. I'm an invalid, not an idiot."

Abby pressed the palms of her hands to her eyes. "Can't we do this tomorrow?"

"When?" her father asked. "I'm very busy during the morning; you've got work to do. I thought now would be the perfect time to go over everything we need. It's quiet; no distractions."

"That's because it's the middle of the night."

"Time is of the essence."

"How about we have dinner together tomorrow night? We can discuss it then."

The functioning part of The Doctor's face betrayed his disappointment. Abby knew when she was defeated.

Forty-five minutes later, Abby and her horticultural shopping list were on their way back to bed. Unfortunately, they didn't make it that far. On her way through the living room, Abby froze in her steps. Someone was outside one of the windows.

"Unbelievable!" Abby grabbed one of her father's fiercer looking golf clubs from the hall closet and raced out the back door. "Two nights in a row? Doesn't anyone sleep anymore?"

"Get the hell away from my house you parasite," she screamed as she swung for the guy's head. It would have been an inspired moment had she made contact, but, alas, aim was never one of Abigail Gardner's strong points. The club landed in the shrubbery and Abby on her ass. The man whose head she had attempted to sever with her old man's driver had made some sort of martial arts-like move for her mid-section when he saw her coming.

As she lay in the wet grass that early morning waiting for the ability to exhale to return, Abby came to the realization that in retrospect, the more prudent idea might have been to have simply dialed 911.

Ever the efficient watchdog, Maggie strolled out to see what was going on. She sniffed Abby, peed, and then walked over to warmly greet the creature who had slammed her arch-nemesis to the ground.

"All right, miss," the man said, petting Maggie. "You want to tell me exactly what you're doing here?"

"What I'm doing here?" Abby gasped painfully as her breath began to return. "What I'm doing here? I live here. What the hell are you doing here?"

"I'm working," he said as he helped Abby sit up.

"Really? It's somewhat late for the gardener, don't you think?"

"I'm not here for the lawn. I'm watching the house. I work for Howard Smileowitz."

"One of Smileowitz's gorillas. Great."

"I prefer the term goon, myself, ma'am. I was told you had some trouble out here last night."

"Something like that." Abby looked at the man who had moments ago made her one with her lawn. In the moonlight he didn't appear to be a hired killer. He looked vaguely familiar. "Don't I know you?"

Smileowitz's muscle shined a flashlight in Abby's face. "Abby?" he asked.

"Yeah," she said, shielding her eyes. "Who are you?"

"You don't remember me?" He held the flashlight under his chin. It appeared to be a nice face, even with red light shining up his nostrils. "Danny Morello."

"Danny Morello?" Abby repeated. "Why do I know that name?"

"We went to high school together."

Abby was drawing a blank. "Don't take it personally, but I spent years in therapy trying to block out as much of my high school experience as I possibly could."

"I'm still working on repressing the memories myself. But it's not that easy to tuck four years of life as a hundred-and-ten pound human punching bag with bad skin into your subconscious."

"I remember you. You look a lot different than you did in high school."

"It's amazing what a late puberty can do," he said, helping her to her feet.

Abby and Danny caught up on the basics as they sat in the Gardner family kitchen polishing off the remains of an incredible strudel Olga had created. Dressed in jeans, a black tee-shirt and sporting sideburns, Danny Morello had that scraggly, out-of-work-musician look about him. He told Abby he was a former cop, and had been working for Howard Smileowitz part time for about a year.

"I'm starting law school at Georgetown in the fall."

"Former cop?" Abby sensed a good story.

"I decided it was time for a change."

"Why was that?"

"Because I got shot."

"Really?"

"It's not all that exciting."

Danny told Abby that he had been accidentally shot while sitting at a desk in the station house.

"Another officer was cleaning his gun in the next room and it discharged. Went through a wall and right through my chest."

"Through your chest?" Abby asked.

"Through and through. Came out my back. Doctor said I was the luckiest son-of-a-bitch he'd ever seen. Missed my heart by this much." Danny held his thumb and forefinger about two inches apart. "I took it as a sign."

"I'll bet you did."

ABBY MADE IT BACK to bed shortly after four A.M. She managed to grab about fifty minutes of sleep before she was awakened again, this time by Smileowitz and one of his all too regular pre-dawn phone calls. She was beginning to think she got more sleep when she was working for "The Journal."

"I want to talk to your brother again about this Dawson piece of crap."

"You're his attorney, Smileowitz. I don't think you need to get my permission to talk to him."

"I'm not looking for your friggin' permission, Gardner. I'm looking for your assistance. You can yank information out of him far more efficiently than I can. I think this Dawson guy is a complete fraud and I'm sure your brother knows a lot more about him than what he's told us. I want you to talk to him about it with me; get him to at least point us in the right direction."

"We don't have to do it right now, do we?"

"No, I want you to meet me over at the jail at eleven."

Abby looked over at the clock. "Then why the hell did you call me at five?"

"Cause I like hearing your voice when you're sleepy. It's husky and sexy, starts my day on a good note. See you later."

ABBY TRIED TO SLEEP for a few more hours, but gave up shortly before eight when the noise of The Doctor and his therapist going through their morning routine started to make the floors vibrate. She showered, dressed and headed off on her gardening expedition. When she returned, her father refused to continue with his physical therapy until he checked each individual plant Abby had purchased.

"Excellent, Abigail, excellent!" The Doctor exclaimed as he examined each seedling. "This afternoon we plant!"

"I've got research to do this afternoon."

"Tomorrow, then."

"I'm not sure if I can, I have a lot of work tomorrow, too."

"Well, we can do it early, before you start working."

"Maybe Hudson can help you with it."

"I don't know."

Again, Abby could see the disappointment on his face. She found the whole concept mind-boggling. This was a man who's child rearing credo was "I'm your father, not your friend," a man who would schedule dinner with his kids through his secretary, a man who believed children should be neither seen nor heard, and now he was disappointed because his daughter didn't want to garden with him? Charles Gardner had been growing his vegetables solo for all twenty-eight of Abby's years. Then he has a stroke and suddenly he wants company?

"I guess Hudson and I could manage it without you," The Doctor said, turning his eyes toward the ground.

Abby was amazed. "Jesus, so this is what parental guilt is like. We can start tomorrow at seven. I'm so glad I'm out of work so I can get some sleep."

"You know that I don't like it when you swear, Abigail."

Abby muttered an apology. She looked at her father's face. The half he had control over was smiling. Abby had to admit it--this dutiful daughter thing did have it moments.

TWELVE

"I DON'T UNDERSTAND exactly what it is that you are asking me," Bennett said as he sat in his usual chair in the jail visitor's room. He was smoking a cigarette and studying his fingernails. Abby could tell from the tone of her brother's voice that he was in a mood.

Howard Smileowitz stomped around the small room. "I want you to explain to me exactly why we shouldn't believe this guy."

Bennett looked up at the ceiling and exhaled a cloud of smoke. "Explain to me why you should?"

"Jesus! Why does everyone in your family insist on answering every fucking question with another question?"

"It's a sign of intelligence," Bennett snorted.

"Oh yeah smart boy? Then why don't you use some of that intelligence to explain to me why we, and the rest of the free world, shouldn't believe what Campbell Dawson has to say?"

"Because Campbell Dawson is full of shit. And if my attorney is not perceptive enough to see that, I'm in even more trouble than I thought was in."

Howard Smileowitz pulled a chair up close to his client and sat down. "Campbell Dawson is so full of shit his breath attracts flies."

"Gosh, Abby," Bennett said. "You didn't tell me he was a poet, too."

"Cut it out, Bennett." Abby was exhausted from the previous evening's activities and in no mood for games. "He's trying to help you."

Bennett took another drag on his cigarette. "If he was with Emily, there's got to be something fucked up there."

"Why?" Smileowitz asked.

Bennett shrugged.

Abby took a seat across the table from her brother. "You've got to give us something to go on. We need to discredit this guy. According to him you had a definite motive for wanting Emily Boyle dead."

"That's bullshit."

"What about Cassandra?" Abby asked. "She was close with Emily. She must have known how her sister felt about you."

"I'm sure she did, but good luck finding her or getting her to talk to you."

"I thought you said she liked you?" Abby asked.

"She did, but she's still a Boyle."

"Let's worry about Cassandra later," Smileowitz interrupted. "First explain to me why Emily wasn't going to marry this guy."

"Trust me," Bennett said. "She wasn't."

"Why?" Smileowitz asked.

"Because she wasn't. It was always the same deal with Em. She wasn't going to marry him."

"Maybe this one was different," Abby suggested.

"I doubt it," Bennett scoffed.

"But how can you be sure?" Smileowitz asked. "How can you be positive she wasn't going to toss you over for this guy?"

"Because she threatened to do it before," Bennett said angrily.

"What was the fight about?" Abby asked.

"What?" Bennett asked, turning his attention from his lawyer to his sister.

"The fight you had the night she died," Abby said. "What was it about?"

"We always fought," Bennett said, putting his cigarette out on the bottom of his shoe.

"Yeah," Smileowitz said. "But I'm assuming most of those fights ended with both you and Emily still breathing."

"Fuck you," Bennett said.

"Was the fight about Dawson?" Abby asked trying to maintain her good cop tone.

Bennett shrugged.

"Please," Abby pleaded with her brother. "You've got to help us here. You've got to give us something to go with."

Bennett looked at his sister. His tone softened a bit. "The fight wasn't about Campbell Dawson, at least not directly. Emily wanted to get married, but I didn't think it was the best idea."

"Why not?" Smileowitz asked.

"We would kill each other. I loved Emily, but I knew it wouldn't work. Our personalities, the worst aspects of our personalities, were too much alike. We were like an extended head-on train crash."

It was one of Bennett's rare displays of mature and reasonable thinking.

"The night she died, Emily told me that she wanted to get married. It wasn't the first time she'd brought it up. We had spent the day arguing about it. She talked about ending things with me because I didn't want to marry her. She said there were others who wanted her."

"What did you tell her?" Smileowitz asked.

"I told her she wasn't going to bully me into marrying her. That went over real big."

"I can imagine," Abby said.

"We fought for a while, we went out, we fought some more. She was totally wired that night."

"What do you mean 'wired?'" Smileowitz asked.

"Wired, crazy," Bennett said slowly, as if talking to a moron.

"Cocaine?" Smileowitz asked.

"She knew I didn't want her near that shit."

"You're saying she didn't use it?" Smileowitz asked.

"No, I'm saying she didn't use it around me."

"So what was she wired on?" Abby asked.

"I suppose it could have been drugs," Bennett said. "But sometimes Emily was just nuts on her own, no chemical additives necessary."

"But you didn't see her do any drugs that night?" Smileowitz asked.

"No, I didn't, but she wouldn't have done them in front of me."

Smileowitz paused to take this in. Bennett's insistence that Emily wasn't high the night she died certainly wasn't going to make defending him any easier. "So," Smileowitz said, changing the subject. "She wanted you to marry her?"

"She wouldn't leave it alone. She told me about Dawson. I told her it didn't make a difference."

"Did you hit her?" Smileowitz asked.

Bennett looked offended. "Of course not."

"Then do you want to explain the internal bleeding that caused her death, and the scratches on your arms?"

"She came after me," Bennett insisted.

"And you hit her defending yourself?" Smileowitz asked.

"I never hit her," Bennett said again.

"So what did you do?" Smileowitz asked. "Stand there with your arms at your side while she pounded the crap out of you?"

"Basically," Bennett said reaching for another cigarette.

"And you never accidentally popped her while you were standing there not fending her off?" Smileowitz asked.

"No, I didn't," Bennett said, lighting the cigarette.

Smileowitz looked at his client. "If you say so."

"Look," Abby said, defending Bennett. "There are very few things you can't say about my brother, but trust me he'd never lay a hand on anyone."

"Thank you," Bennett said.

"Did she attack you often?" Smileowitz asked.

"She didn't attack me. She would get physical when she got frustrated or angry. She'd push me or something. I assumed it was the way things were done in the Boyle household. I wasn't a battered boyfriend by any stretch of the imagination, if that's the defense strategy you're concocting."

"Not really," Smileowitz said. "But I'm not ruling anything out."

RETURNING HOME FROM visiting her brother, Abby was once again forced to run a gauntlet of reporters and photographers. They had turned the street in front of her father's house into some sort of outdoor encounter group for chain smokers and caffeine junkies. They yelled questions at her as she drove past their encampment, but as was her custom, she ignored them all.

Once inside, she made a phone call she was dreading. It took calls to "The Journal," his cell phone, and a couple of bars before she was able to locate Markham.

"I need you to do me a favor," Abby said, almost gagging on the words.

"For you, love, anything."

She could tell from the way he was slurring his words he'd been at the bar for a while. "I want you to do a story."

"You'll have to be more specific, my dear," Markham said.

"I want you to do a story on Campbell Dawson." Abby had debated the ethics of suggesting a segment involving her brother's case to her coworkers. After much consideration, she decided that there was nothing wrong with her nudging them in the direction of a possible story. As long as they didn't make anything up, and got an actual news piece out of it, what was the harm?

"What have you got?" Markham asked.

"Not much. Just a hunch."

Markham laughed. "Bloody hell, I've done hour-long specials that started with less than that."

"Dawson says he's from Chicago, but my brother said Emily told him that he's really from outside of Wausau, Wisconsin."

"Bennett knew about him?"

Abby paused. "I don't want to get into it."

"Listen, love, fair is fair."

Great, Abby thought. She wanted to keep her input on this to an untraceable minimum. "Yeah he knew about him. Apparently, discretion wasn't always Emily's strong suit."

Abby told Markham just enough of what she knew to make him happy and willing. "I've got a feeling that Mr. Dawson isn't really what he seems, and it might be nice to see some investigative press on him. It might jog some memories."

"I concur entirely," Markham said. "The interviews I've seen have been pathetic. During that piece of refuse "American Magazine" put together, he was practically sitting in Joely Rogan's exquisite little lap."

"I know something's not right with the guy, and I'm only asking you to check it out because I'm in no position to go nosing around after him myself."

"I understand completely."

"Please, keep it on the level."

"Abigail, if I wasn't positive that was your tortured emotions talking, I'd be insulted."

"Please," Abby repeated.

"Define 'level,'" Markham laughed as he hung up the phone.

DINNER THAT NIGHT with The Doctor was quiet. They ate in his room where he peppered her with questions about Bennett and seemed to listen intently to her answers. After he fell asleep Abby retired to the living room to watch the evening news programs alone.

"The Report" had a woman who professed to have been a nanny and housekeeper for the Gardner children during the early seventies. Abby had never seen her before in her life which made her claim that she relieved Bennett of his virginity at the tender age of twelve somewhat difficult for her to believe.

"Late Edition" scored even higher on the sensational scale. They managed to locate a young woman named Lauren Cole, an aspiring actress who claimed she and Bennett were a hot item for several months before he'd met Emily Boyle, and she had the photographs to prove it.

"Late Edition's" entire show focused on Ms. Cole's fascinating story. Most of the program took place poolside in Los Angeles where Lauren had moved to pursue her career. The program included a clip of her recent guest appearance on the syndicated action/drama "Jet Ski Patrol" where most of her emoting was done in a tiny, wet bikini.

"We did an egregious amount of drugs together," Lauren confessed to "Late Edition's" correspondent. "Pot, cocaine. It was a really bad time for me. My head was so not-together. We drank a lot, too. It was out of hand. I had to get away from him."

The interview quickly segued to their sex life.

"Bennett was a remarkable lover," she explained. "Very unselfish, very imaginative, very adventurous."

"But didn't your lovemaking sometimes have a dark side, Lauren?" the reporter asked.

"Bennett did have some strange tastes. He would often hit me and the sex would get rough, especially if we were high, which was most of the time. He liked to tie me to the bed, he really got into that, but I found it very frightening." She began to cry without smudging any of her makeup.

Abby thought Lauren Cole and Gwen Mason must shop at the same waterproof cosmetics counter.

The reporter leaned forward and touched her knee. "Are you all right?"

Lauren nodded and wiped away a tear. "I'll be okay. I try to use the pain, you know, channel it into my work."

The most remarkable part of the Lauren Cole story, however, wasn't even on "Late Edition." It aired on "The Journal." Abby couldn't imagine what Markham and Gordon must have coughed up to get the information about "Late Edition's" story before it hit the airwaves, but they took what they knew and ran straight to Howard

Smileowitz. Abby was very impressed with the interview. Smileowitz, looking every inch the commanding criminal defense attorney, spoke with Markham in his shiny, black office. He told "The Journal" that "Late Edition" obviously didn't do their research.

"Using minimal investigative effort, the average junior high school newspaper would have been able to locate several other young men who had been involved with Ms. Cole and some of her rather unusual, yet perfectly legal proclivities. My client, Bennett Gardner, admits he was briefly involved with this young woman, but is adamant that he never hit her. Three other men I've spoken with, though, have told me that they did indeed participate in so-called rough sex with Ms. Cole. They have all assured me that these sex acts were always initiated by Ms. Cole, and that the only blows, so to speak, that were struck in these relationships were in the form of spanking, an activity that Ms. Cole seemed to be particularly fond of."

To confirm Smileowitz's allegations, "The Journal" interviewed Andrew Kohler, a public relations executive in his mid-thirties who did not seem to be overburdened with brains.

"Lauren was totally into the spanking thing," he told the reporter. "She liked me to put her over my knee. Afterwards she would call me 'daddy' and insist on having peanut-butter and jelly sandwiches with milk."

But the story that really caught Abby's attention that night was on "American Magazine," which had recently expanded to two nights a week to give the Emily Boyle murder all the network coverage it deserved. Their report featured another brief interview with Thomas Boyle.

Instead of speaking from his attorney's office as he usually did, Boyle sat down with Joely Rogan in the family-photo-filled living room of his Georgetown townhouse. Instead of his usual suit and tie, Boyle wore an open-collared shirt and a cardigan. It made Abby wonder what the little media monster was up to.

She didn't have to wonder for long. After a few brief pleasantries they got to the point.

"What do you want to see happen with this case?" Joely asked.

"I'm torn, Joely. I'm honestly torn."

"How so?"

"As an attorney and a Justice Department official I would like nothing more than to see Bennett Gardner prosecuted to the fullest extent of the law, but as a brother and a grandson and a human being I would like to avoid the trauma of sensational trial and put this matter to rest as quickly as possible. I would be pleased to see Bennett Gardner and the Sussex County District Attorney's Office reach a plea agreement."

This guy is unbelievable, Abby thought. He could fertilize the North American wheat crop for a decade with the crap he was spewing.

"That's quite a departure from your earlier statements, Mr. Boyle. Why the change?"

Boyle paused for effect before answering. "It's because of my family. Or what's left of my family. My younger sister, Cassandra, my only surviving sibling, never knew my mother and barely knew my father and my brother before they were taken from us. Emily's death has hit her particularly hard and I'd like to spare her the additional trauma that a sensational trial would add. Then there is my Grandmother Margaret, who turned ninety-six this past April."

"A woman loved and admired by many Americans," Joely added.

"Yes, but a woman who has endured more than her share of tragedy during her lifetime. She is strong as an ox, always has been, but Emily's death has been too much for her to bear. Personally, I would love nothing more than to see Bennett Gardner in court and watch our justice system at work. But it is because of my sister and my grandmother that I hope Mr. Gardner's case never sees the inside of a courtroom. It is for both of them that I want to avoid the torture of what is sure to be a very, very public trial."

"WAS I BRILLIANT, or was I brilliant?" Howard Smileowitz bellowed into the phone when he called early the next morning. "I'd have told you about the story, but your brother and your pal Markham wanted to surprise you. They thought you'd love the piece."

"I did enjoy it," Abby said, yawning. She glanced at the clock. Smileowitz had actually let her sleep past six. "But I am a bit more concerned with Thomas Boyle's statements to the press last night than ours."

Smileowitz laughed. "Seems like the little bastard is frightened of something. Did you believe that crap about his grandmother? What a heap of bull feces. He'd push that old woman off a cliff any day of the week if he thought she'd cushion his fall."

"My thoughts, exactly. If Boyle wants to avoid the publicity of a trial, it's not to spare anyone, including his own beloved, aging granny any pain. If he's willing to toss away all the sympathetic attention that his sister's death has foisted upon him and his political career, there has to be something he wants to keep within the family."

"Well, Gardner," Smileowitz said, "your job now is to figure out what that something might be."

THIRTEEN

"HOW'S IT GOING?" Danny Morello asked as he made his way around the rear of the Gardner homestead checking for intruders.

Abby was sitting on the steps of the back porch, drinking coffee and watching the moonlight dance across the waters of Long Island Sound. "Not great," she told him.

Her day had started out well. No one woke her at five. There was no busy-work for her to do, no pointless research designed to simply keep her out of Howard Smileowitz's slicked-back hair. Instead she finally had something to do that could actually help her brother's case. Now, she would see some results. Thomas Boyle was trying to avoid a very public trial and it was Abby's assigned task to discover why. It took her eight fruitless hours of pouring over her collection of Boyle family materials to realize she had no idea how she was going to find out what Boyle wanted to keep quiet.

"I'm trying to save my brother's ass," Abby told Danny. "And it's not going all that well."

"I can't imagine it's too easy a task."

"No, it's not. But my brother didn't do this. He's innocent. I know people say that all the time, but he really is."

"If you say so," Danny said, nudging some dirt around with the toe of his black canvas sneaker.

Abby sensed he was trying to be kind. As a former cop he had probably heard thousands of guilty people protest their innocence. "You don't know Bennett," she said, "but he's incapable of doing what they've accused him of. He's an irresponsible idiot, but he's totally harmless. He wouldn't hurt a fly."

"Okay." Danny smiled at her.

She liked the look in his eyes. "You believe me?"

"It's more like I'm giving you the benefit of the doubt."

Abby took a sip of her coffee. "Your pal, Smileowitz, has me checking into the extensive saga of the Boyles."

"What are you looking for?"

"We think Thomas Boyle may be hiding something."

"Like what?"

Abby shrugged.

"Well, Smileowitz is the best. I'm sure he knows what he's doing."

"I sure hope so," Abby said. "Because I haven't found anything yet that even remotely relates to my brother's case."

"Well, if Bennett is innocent like you say, there wouldn't be. You have to be looking for something that relates to Emily Boyle's death, not your brother."

Abby thought about it for a second. He had a point.

"THE JOURNAL'S" STORY on Campbell Dawson aired two days later. Markham put it together with a producer named Gayle Klein, and Abby thought they did an admirable job.

The piece focused on the same Mr. Dawson who, with the help of two major networks, had captured the heart and interest of a nation, although there were a few differences. The Campbell Dawson of "American Magazine" and "The World This Evening's" was a sophisticated, Ivy League investment banker from Chicago with country club credentials. Markham and Klein had discovered that Dawson had only adopted the "P" in Campbell in recent years. They soon realized the old spelling wasn't the only part of his past that Dawson wanted to leave behind.

The P-less Cambell Dawson hailed from the diminutive dairy town of Westlake, Wisconsin. Dawson's Uncle Wayne assured "The Journal's" viewing audience that the closest his nephew ever got to the Ivy League was accidentally driving through Boston in the family camper after a disappointing fourth place finish in the Junior New England Cheese Festival.

"Cammy was a funny little boy," Uncle Wayne said flipping through the family photo album with Markham. They were seated on folding beach chairs on Wayne's front porch. "He was always cracking jokes, always laughing, always trying on his mother's shoes. He sure loved those sling-backs."

According to Uncle Wayne, "Little Cammy" *did* attend business college in Wisconsin, and then moved to Chicago where he "traded something, but we were never quite sure what."

BLOOD RELATIONS

The Securities and Exchange Commission seemed to have some questions about exactly what Cambell-without-the-P Dawson was trading, as well. According to Markham's sources at the S.E.C., Dawson was stealing from all but two of his clients in order to support his two-thousand-dollar-a-week cocaine habit. The Cook County Prosecutor's Office happily informed him that Dawson was married to both of the other two clients simultaneously, and that he now owed one of his two former co-wives close to forty-thousand dollars in back child support.

Abby slept better that night than she had in weeks.

THE FOLLOWING EVENING, Abby told Danny that she had decided to take his advice and started looking into the Boyle clan.

Danny joined her as she enjoyed her after-dinner coffee down by the beach. The place where the Long Island Sound met the eastern-most point of the Gardner backyard was one of Abby's favorite places on the planet. She had spent countless hours during her childhood staring out at the softly rolling water, contemplating life.

She had occupied most of her day re-examining everything she had found on the Boyles, looking for any scrap of information that might have something to do with Emily's death.

"Did you find anything?" Danny asked.

Abby shook her head. "Not exactly," she said, happy to have another person around the house to speak with besides her father. Danny asked her what she had come up with, and she told him the Boyles seem to share a few common threads.

"Such as?" he asked.

"Well," she said taking a sip of her coffee. "They are all Boyles."

Danny smiled. "You are quite the skilled investigator, aren't you?"

"They were all good-looking and wealthy."

"And?"

"And a number of them expired before their time."

"If I was looking for an avenue to pursue, I'd opt for number three," Danny said.

"It's obvious that's where the answers lie," Abby agreed. "The four most recent deaths took place years apart, under completely different circumstances, and were entirely unrelated by any element except for the decedent's last name."

"I'd rule out a serial killer, but I think it's worth further investigation."

Abby told Danny she was also going to try to find Cassandra Boyle. "I figure if there's some big family secret out there, Thomas can't be the only one who knows about it."

"You think she'd talk to you?"

Abby shrugged. "Probably not, but it's worth a shot. Bennett said she liked him, and she was close with Emily. If she knew how much her sister loved him maybe it's worth something."

FOURTEEN

"EXCELLENT, ABIGAIL," THE Doctor said. "Excellent."

Abby had spent the better part of two hours the following morning crawling around in the dirt on her hands and knees planting her father's vegetable garden and listening to him sing her praises. Maggie had christened the event early on by squatting down next to Abby in the vegetable patch and peeing on her sneaker. She then joined her master in the shade and fell asleep.

Abby could take the dirt, even the dog urine, but her father's enthusiasm was making her uneasy. He was sitting in his wheelchair, humming "Oliver," and watching Abby's every move.

"You are doing a tremendous job," he said. "Just tremendous."

This was getting to be too much for Abby. This was the man who said nothing when she skipped the eighth grade. He had no comment when she graduated from high school at sixteen and headed for the Ivy League. He had no words of praise when she graduated with honors from Columbia University, nor when she landed a job on a national television program. However, when it came to her vegetable garden assembly skills, this made him proud.

"Are you going to continue with your research today?" The Doctor asked Abby as she showed him a tomato plant prior to planting it.

"As soon as I'm done here," she told him.

"Have you found anything helpful yet?"

"No," she said, annoyed. "Not much." This was definitely not a line of questioning she wished to continue with her father. She was dismayed enough with her lack of progress; discussing it with The Doctor would only make her feel worse.

"Well, I'm positive if there *is* something there to find, you will uncover it."

Great, Abby thought to herself. That makes one of us.

"Miss Gardner!" Olga bellowed, walking towards them waving the portable telephone. "You have a telephone call."

Abby was happy to have both the conversation and her gardening interrupted. She met Olga halfway across the lawn.

"It is that Markham person," Olga announced with great displeasure as she handed over the phone. Then she went to check on The Doctor.

"By any chance does that Prussian House Frau of yours wear one of those starched white uniforms, the kind that creaks its own lovely melody as she walks?" Markham asked.

Abby ignored Markham's nursing fantasies. "I was going to call you this afternoon," she said. "I have something I need to talk to you about."

"Why don't you meet me at The Red Hat around lunch time? I have something I think you might be interested in as well."

"Oh yeah?" Abby asked.

"Trust me, love, it behooves you to meet me."

THE RED HAT WAS another one of Markham's favorite hangouts. Abby knew he had a preferred bar for each square block in Manhattan.

By the time she got to The Red Hat at one, Markham had already set up camp in a corner of the bar. He welcomed her with a degree of eloquence and gusto that let Abby know he had been there since they opened. Abby sat down next to him and ordered a club soda.

"Why don't you ask me what you need first," Markham said, "and then I'll dazzle you with what I've uncovered."

"I want to find Cassandra Boyle," Abby said.

Markham laughed. "Good luck, love. Garbo would call that young woman standoff-ish."

"I was thinking of starting with Janet Evans," Abby said after the bartender brought her drink.

Janet Evans' was "The Journal's" Senior Entertainment Correspondent. She specialized in celebrity gossip, and Abby figured she might have some information on Cassandra's known hangouts.

Markham nodded. "Good idea. I'd also check with Gayle Klein. She's done most of our Boyle stories, even before this latest round, she's pretty well versed on the subject."

"I'll give her a call. What's this other thing you've found that you're so sure I'd be interested in?"

Markham reached into his jacket pocket and removed a thick white envelope, placed it on the bar and slid it towards her. Abby picked it up warily. Markham was grinning like he had recently ingested a gross of canaries. He was awfully proud of whatever was in the envelope and, knowing Markham as she did, that made Abby uneasy. Inside, she found several lined pages stapled together. Upon further examination, Abby discovered that the papers were medical records, Emily Boyle's medical records.

"Geez," Abby said, whistling in admiration. She was constantly amazed at what Markham could get his hands on.

"Impressive, isn't it?" Markham whispered. "Amazing what a few well placed currency notes can get you."

"I was hoping you hadn't bought them," Abby said, putting the file down in front of Markham. She didn't want to know where the papers had come from.

"Actually," Markham said, nudging the folder towards her, "I only rented them. I have to give them back tonight and I promised not to make any copies. The family physician who scribbled them died about five years ago. These were borrowed from his estate."

Abby stared at the folder sitting on the bar. "How long do I have to commit them to memory?"

"That depends entirely on how much beer money you have with you."

Abby ran a tab for Markham and began to read, furiously taking notes.

The file indicated in barely-legible physician penmanship that Emily Boyle was vaccinated against all the usual childhood diseases. She had chicken pox when she was five, broke her left arm when she was six and was first referred to a psychiatrist at the ripe old age of nine. The doctor helpfully noted several extended stays at a rehab hospital in Vermont. Emily's first visit to the David-Kilb Clinic in Bennington was when she was fourteen. According to the file, Emily was allergic to penicillin and had inherited her mother's hay fever, asthma, blue eyes and, apparently, some sort of hat.

An odd notation, but Abby figured the doctor must been very fond of Mrs. Boyle's millinery choices.

Ninety minutes later Markham had somehow consumed nine beers and Abby had copied everything she needed to know from a private medical file she had no right to see.

At this point she was in no position to take the high road.

"THIS IS TOTAL BULLSHIT. I am going to drive up to Bennington tomorrow."

"The hell you are."

Abby was having a late night snack with Howard Smileowitz at a diner in Yonkers where apparently no one ever sat with their back towards the door. "It's my lead."

"Yeah," Smileowitz said, his mouth full of cheesecake. "And it's also your brother's ass behind bars."

"Exactly."

"You're talking crazy, Gardner. I can't have the sister of the accused traipsing all over this investigation. We have to appear somewhat professional."

"I am a perfectly capable investigator," Abby said, using her fork to push a piece of half-eaten chocolate cake around her plate.

"I'm sure you are, but you're also the only sibling of the accused. I don't think anyone at the clinic is going to want talk to us to begin with, but I am positive no one will want to talk to you."

Abby pushed her plate away. "This is total bullshit."

"I must be winning this argument." Smileowitz grinned. "You're starting to repeat yourself."

"Do I know you well enough to tell you to fuck off?"

"You're paying me enough to tell me anything you want." Smileowitz signaled the waitress for more coffee. "Look, I know you want to help and I know it's killing you that you aren't able to jump all over this in the style you are accustomed to. But keep in mind we are all working towards the same goal here. You know, saving your brother's neck?"

"Great, so I just keep supplying the leads and you send someone else to do the good stuff?"

"Gardner, could you imagine what would happen if the press found out you were knocking on doors about this? They'd eat you alive. And, truthfully, I don't think the court would be too thrilled about it, either. We can't have you out there talking to potential witnesses. You've got to let us do it."

"HE HAS A POINT."

"I know he has a point, but it still doesn't make me feel any better."

Abby had told Danny that she had reluctantly relinquished the name of the rehab clinic to Smileowitz and that he had forced her to take an oath not to go within a hundred miles of it.

"You've just got to trust Smileowitz with this. Believe me. The guy knows what he's doing." Danny was watching with great interest as Abby whizzed stone after stone into the Long Island Sound. It was a stress relieving technique she had developed years before. Since her return to Easton she had tossed enough pebbles into the water to start a new continent.

"I know," Abby said, tossing another stone. "But I'm just not used to operating this way. It's usually my lead, my story."

"Not much of a team player, huh?"

"I'm just a firm believer in the theory that if you want something done right, you do it yourself."

Danny wiped an imaginary tear from his eye. "While that is a lovely sentiment, you are going to have to learn to function in a slightly different way on this one."

"I don't like relying on other people."

"You don't have much of a choice. You know you can't defend your brother on your own, and it wouldn't be fair to him to try. He's depending on you to do everything you can to help him."

"If you bring my father into this, I swear you'll be sorry."

"I don't think that will be necessary," he said with a mock-serious tone. "I think I've made my point."

"I hate this," Abby said.

"You just have to keep your mind off it."

"And how exactly do I do that?"

"You have to focus on something else. You need to do something you enjoy. What happened to looking into those multiple untimely deaths?"

"I didn't get to it today," Abby sulked. "I was working on something that I thought might actually help the case."

"Well, now, you won't know if those deaths can help until you actually look into them, will you?"

FIFTEEN

ANNE LELAND BOYLE'S death in 1970, immediately after giving
birth to her daughter, Cassandra, generated front page headlines
across the nation. Her demise at age thirty-four was attributed to a
massive cerebral hemorrhage brought on by the trauma of childbirth.
The country was shocked by the sudden passing of a woman who
along with her young family seemed to symbolize youth and vitality.

Her obituary in the *Washington Post* referred to Mrs. Boyle as
"one half of the most famous political couple in the United States,
outside of the President and his wife." The *New York Times* described
her as "a much admired and imitated woman, whose loss would be
mourned not only by her husband and children, but by an entire
nation."

Anne Boyle's premature death only added to the fascination
the public already had with her family, but, for the Boyles, tragedy
was just getting warmed up.

Gilbert Boyle Jr. was killed in December of 1974. His death
orphaned his children and was a crushing blow to a nation already
reeling from war and political disgrace. To many, the young Senator
was a beacon of hope, an idealist in a sea of cynicism. To Gilbert
Boyle Sr. he was the family's best chance to forever enshrine
themselves in the political history of the nation. At the time of his
death, the senator was widely expected to run for president in the
next election. Senator Boyle's vocal opposition to the war in
Vietnam had evolved into a personal mission to make sure that every
American soldier sent to Southeast Asia was somehow accounted
for. He was passionate about his work on behalf of those still missing
or held prisoner in Vietnam. He had made several trips to the region
on behalf of the U.S. Government and the families of American
servicemen who hadn't made it home. It was on one of these

journeys shortly before Christmas of 1974 that the senator and six others were killed when their small plane crashed into the South China Sea.

It was the death of young Gilbert Boyle III in 1973, however, that interested Abby the most. Unfortunately, he was killed before the first shots were fired in the tabloid wars, and information on his death, considering he was a Boyle, was slim.

During the summer of 1973 Senator Boyle had sent his four children to spend the month of July with their maternal grandparents at their summer residence in the scenic beach paradise of Milton, Connecticut. The young Boyles, ranging in age from three to twelve years, spent their leisure-filled summer days sailing or swimming in the pool or down at the beach, or improving their tennis games on the backyard court.

Gilbert Boyle III celebrated his tenth birthday the week he arrived at the Lelands. His father had sent him a chemistry set for the occasion, but it was his grandparents who really came through. They bestowed upon him the keys to a brand new, midnight-blue Schwinn Sting Ray with a banana seat, chopper handle-bars and a horn that would frighten geese.

Young Gilbert fell in love with the bicycle, and while his sisters and brother spent most of their days cooling off in the pool, Gilbert passed his time astride his new bike, exploring the streets of Milton.

According to the papers, it was on one of these rides that he collided with a speeding sedan driven by a postal worker named William Radley.

Gilbert Boyle III died shortly after seven that evening at Shore Hospital. The cause of death was massive internal bleeding brought on by injuries sustained in the accident. William Radley was arrested and charged with reckless driving and vehicular homicide.

The quarter-of-a-century old newspaper photographs accompanying the articles showed an obviously distraught William Radley under arrest, his 1970 Oldsmobile at the scene of the accident, and a police officer wheeling Gilbert Boyle's beloved bicycle into a police van.

Gilbert Boyle Jr. went into seclusion after his young son's death, but a grief-stricken Gilbert Sr. repeatedly vented to the press about the loss of his grandson. He believed William Radley should rot in jail for the rest of his days for what he'd done, and promised that he would use every resource he had to see to it that he did.

Two weeks after Gilbert Boyle III was killed, William Radley pleaded guilty to manslaughter and was sentenced to eight-to-fifteen years in prison. He served ten before being paroled.

By the time Abby had finished reading all she had on the deaths of the Boyles she was exhausted, both mentally and physically. The tragedy went beyond description. Emily's death was only the latest blow to a family already devastated by fate. Her loss was the fourth in thirty years for a family that should have had everything and now was left with only two survivors.

Abby thought about the pain Thomas and Cassandra Boyle must live with on a daily basis. They were all that was left. It made Abby think of her own mother, a woman whom she only knew through photographs and other people's memories. If Bennett was convicted of Emily's murder, she and her father could wind up being the only two surviving Gardners as well.

SIXTEEN

SMILEOWITZ WAITED UNTIL six-fifteen the next morning to call Abby.

"What's the matter?" she asked, holding her pillow over her eyes to block the sunlight. "Get a late start?"

"No, for me it's still last night."

"Well, as long as you're enjoying yourself."

"Not this time." Smileowitz cleared his throat. "Listen, somehow a few of the other inmates got hold of your brother last night."

Abby bolted upright in bed. "Is he alright?"

"They beat him up pretty good, but he's going to be okay."

"Where is he?"

"Sussex County Medical Center."

BY THE TIME Abby made it to the hospital, the press had started arriving. They chased her right up to the front door shouting questions.

Abby ignored all of them. She found Smileowitz in the emergency room waiting area, talking with a couple of deputies.

"Where is he?" she demanded. "Can I see him?

Smileowitz put an arm around Abby's shoulder and gently steered her away from the cops. "They're finishing stitching him up now. You can see him when they're done."

"Have you seen him?" she asked. "Is he okay?"

"He looks like shit," Smileowitz said, shaking his head. "They messed him up pretty good, but the doctor said he'll be fine."

Abby couldn't believe this was happening. "What does 'messed him up pretty good' translate into medically?"

"A couple of broken ribs and a lot of cuts and bruises."

"How the hell did this happen? I thought he was in protective custody?"

"I thought so, too."

"WELL," BENNETT SAID AN hour later when Abby and Smileowitz were allowed to see him, "there go my boyish good looks."

Abby was at a loss for words. Bennett's face was so swollen and bruised that if she didn't know it was her brother, she wouldn't have recognized him. Bandages covered the stitches above his left eye and wrapped around his arm and chest.

"Say something, please," Bennett's voice sounded hoarse. "You're frightening me."

"You don't look so bad," Abby said, trying to smile. "How do you feel?"

"Like someone parked a truck on my chest."

"Great," Abby said.

"After running it over my head," Bennett added.

"What happened?" Smileowitz asked.

"Damned if I know. I was fast asleep, then the next thing I knew I was on the floor and those two simians were beating the crap out of me. I felt like I was back in prep school, except these guys had better-quality tattoos."

"They were in your cell?" Abby asked.

"No, they did this by telekinesis."

Smileowitz laughed. "At least we know he didn't suffer any brain damage."

"What the hell were they doing in your cell? You're supposed to be in protective custody," Abby said.

"You know, I tried to tell them that but they were awfully busy rearranging some of my better features."

"According to the deputies it was some sort of personnel mix-up, some rookie guard crap or something," Smileowitz informed them. "They're still trying to sort it out."

"Bullshit," Bennett said. "Those two animals knew exactly who I was."

"The whole world knows who you are," Smileowitz reminded him.

"Yeah, well these two guys gave me the distinct impression they were trying to send me a message."

"Any message in particular?" Smileowitz asked.

"They seemed very much in favor of me pleading to manslaughter."

"They said that?" Abby asked.

"Not exactly, but while they were taking turns trying to see if my head would dent the wall they mentioned that if I was a smart-rich-fuck like they thought, I'd take the deal. And if I didn't I could expect that the rest of my days in prison would make this one look like the senior prom."

"You didn't go to your senior prom," Abby reminded her brother.

"Again, I tried to explain that to them but they said it was just a goddamn metaphor and I was being too fucking literal."

"Christ," Smileowitz laughed, heading for the door. "I'm glad your parents didn't have any other kids. I'll be back. I'm going to call my office."

"How are you really doing?" Abby asked when they were alone. "Are you in a lot of pain?"

"I'm terrified, Abby. I didn't kill her, but I can't take a lifetime of this."

"You're not going to," Abby assured him.

"You don't know that. You've got to help me. You've got to get me out of here."

ABBY AND SMILEOWITZ stayed with Bennett until the early afternoon when the doctor pronounced him fit enough to return to jail. Smileowitz told Bennett he'd be in the jail infirmary for a couple of days.

"Terrific. I understand it's a satellite facility of Johns Hopkins."

"You'll be okay there," Smileowitz said.

Abby took her brother's hand after they helped him into a wheelchair. "I'll be by tomorrow morning."

"You'll tell the old man I'm okay?"

"I promise."

"And get me out of here, please."

"We're working on it."

"I know you are, just work faster."

ABBY WENT HOME and gingerly told her father what had happened. Each time she had to tell him bad news she feared he was going to have another stroke. This time he looked as if he was going to cry.

"I thought he was in solitary confinement," The Doctor said.

"He was supposed to be in protective custody. They said it was a mistake."

"We've got to get him out of there Abigail."

"I know."

ABBY DIDN'T EVEN flinch when the phone rang the next morning at five.

"Smileowitz?" she asked without opening her eyes.

"Good morning, sunshine," he laughed into the phone.

"Please tell me you're calling with good news this morning."

"My guy made pals with a janitor at Vermont's answer to The Betty Ford Center. Emily Boyle's last visit was eight weeks ago."

"Great," Abby said, sitting up in bed. "Now at least we know for sure that two months ago she was still indulging in behavior that required rehabilitation."

"Pretty much," Smileowitz said.

"Now, we just need to find someone else who can tell us not only that she was still doing drugs, but that she still owed someone a lot of money for them."

"Yeah," Smileowitz said. "And if that same person could also tell us that they not only witnessed the killing, but videotaped it, that would be a big help, too."

"Well, it's a start," Abby said defensively.

"Yes," he agreed. "It certainly is."

ABBY WAS TOO EXCITED after Smileowitz's phone call to go back to sleep. She met him at the jail at nine to talk to Bennett about what they'd found out.

"If Emily Boyle was in a rehab facility two months before she died, it adds a bit more credence to our theory that one of her druggie associates might have been looking for her when you ran out to get dinner that night," Smileowitz told them.

"I didn't know anything about her being at a clinic," Bennett said.

Abby thought her brother sounded a lot better than he did the day before, but he still looked terrible. She was seated at his bedside in the prison infirmary. There were two other beds in the room, but both were empty.

"How could you not know?" Smileowitz asked as he stood at the foot of Bennett's bed.

"I told you. She didn't do drugs in front of me, or around me. She knew how I felt about it."

"She didn't do rehab in front of you either?" Smileowitz asked.

"No, she didn't." Bennett glared at his lawyer with his blackened eyes.

"She wouldn't have told you if she was going to get help?" Abby asked.

"She told me she wasn't doing drugs, so why would she tell me she was going to get help for them? Besides, did you ever think whoever did this might have been looking for Gwen?"

Smileowitz assured Bennett that they were exploring that aspect as well.

"Where did she tell you she was when this guy says she was at the clinic?" Abby asked.

"She told me she was in London."

"With Dawson?" Abby asked.

"I assumed so. You do realize that she could have been at that clinic, if she was actually there, for any of a number of reasons."

"Such as?" Smileowitz asked.

"Such as she had been there before, she might have enjoyed it, she might have gone to relax, or, or maybe she might have just wanted to talk to someone."

"I like my theory better," Smileowitz said.

"And what theory would that would be?" Bennett asked.

"That she went because she had a problem with cocaine, and when she got back home, one her former suppliers was upset over losing her business, or maybe she didn't settle her tab. He was mad enough to kill her. Sound plausible?"

"She told me she wasn't doing drugs anymore," Bennett repeated. Flexibility wasn't a strong Gardner family trait.

"Any chance she might have been hiding it from you?" Abby asked.

Bennett attempted to shrug, but wound up wincing in pain.

"We're not trying to hurt her," Abby told him. "We're just trying to help you. If Emily was still messed up with drugs when she was killed, it would help us to establish an alternative theory on how this might have happened."

"And how exactly would we do that?" Bennett asked.

"We need the names of people that she used to hang out with. People who would know where she got the drugs," Smileowitz said.

"You think her idiot, druggie friends are going to tell you who killed her?" Bennett scoffed.

"No," Smileowitz said. "I just want them to tell me that someone else besides you might have wanted her dead. It's a quaint little legal concept we like to call reasonable doubt."

Abby and Smileowitz left the jail that morning with the names of several of Emily Boyle's friends who might have more of an intimate knowledge of her drug use than Bennett did.

Smileowitz let Abby look at the list briefly, and then told her to forget all about them. She wasn't going to be allowed anywhere near these potential witnesses either.

AFTER SHE LEFT Bennett, Abby spent an hour on the phone with "The Journal's" gossip reporter, Janet Evans, a person who under normal circumstances Abby took extensive measures to avoid.

Janet, who favored extremely short animal-print skirts and plastic surgery, claimed to be in her late thirties, but Abby guessed she was actually closer to fifty. Her hair was so bleached blonde that it approached translucence, and it was styled and shellacked in such a manner that when she turned her head sometimes the coif wouldn't go with it.

Abby had unwillingly done several interviews for Janet during her tenure with "The Journal." They were often assigned by Gordon at the very last minute, thus giving Abby little opportunity to find a way out. Janet's so-called "pick-up" interviews usually began with a paid interview or a celebrity ambush. They usually concluded with Abby getting spat upon.

Janet knew her stuff, though, and after Gordon ordered her to tell Abby what she wanted, she shared what knowledge she had of Cassandra Boyle's travel habits.

"It's summertime-ish, so I would say possibly Newport, possibly Sag Harbor, possibly The Vineyard."

"That's a lot of possiblies," Abby pointed out.

Janet sighed. "You do realize mine is not an exact science. Also, possibly Europe."

"Great," Abby said.

"I really haven't heard much about her recently, I suspect she's hiding. I know if I were her I certainly would."

ABBY MET GAYLE KLEIN for a late lunch at The Ocean Club. She was a lot more help than Janet.

"Cassandra Boyle is a real mystery," Gayle told her. "She keeps an extremely low profile."

"So I've heard."

Gayle had been with "The Journal" for about a year and a half. She was short with glasses and a lot of flaming-red curly hair that she wore pulled away from her face in a barrette. She also talked incredibly fast.

"What do you want to find her for?"

Abby opted to go with the truth. "I think Thomas Boyle is hiding something that might help my brother."

"And you think Cassandra knows what it is?"

"It's one of the theories I'm playing with."

Gayle seemed doubtful Cassandra would talk to anyone, let alone Abby, but she agreed to help. Luckily, her vast body of work on the Boyles had yielded several highly coveted pieces of information, including the addresses of the Boyle's homes in Newport and Sag Harbor. She also had data on a Fifth Avenue apartment that allegedly belonged to Cassandra Boyle, as well as the hotels she frequented in France, Italy and Switzerland.

"I also had one of the P.A.'s run a Nexus search for any newspaper or magazine articles that mentioned her during the last six months." Gayle removed a short stack of papers from her bag and handed them to Abby. "There's not much, but you might as well go through it."

"This is great." Abby quickly scanned the pages as their lunch arrived.

The Ocean Club was famous for two things--Markham's legendary tab, and its Cobb salad. It was served in a bowl the size of a kiddy pool.

"How's your brother doing?" Gayle asked Abby as they dug into their lunches.

"Are we talking on the record or off?"

"I'm not digging for information," Gayle assured her. "I'm making an attempt at pleasant conversation."

"Sorry, but I'm somewhat out of practice with being gracious to fellow members of the working press. He's doing about as well as can be expected, but it's difficult."

"I can imagine."

Abby was prepared to fend off a barrage of questions about her brother, but instead Gayle asked how her father was doing.

"He had a stroke, didn't he?"

"Yes," Abby said, "he's doing pretty well. Thanks for asking."

"My grandmother had a stroke about two years ago. She's getting along much better now, but it was rough for a while. She walks with a cane, and she's still goes to physical therapy, but her speech is almost completely back to normal."

"My father is still in a wheelchair, but I think his speech gets better every day."

"You're staying with him, right?"

"Yeah."

"Sounds like you have your hands full."

"It's been a little much," Abby admitted.

"Well, if I can help you out with anything else--you know, any information-just give me a call."

"I NEED TO BORROW one of your investigators," Abby informed Howard Smileowitz. "Maybe several."

Abby went to see her brother's attorney after lunch.

"Might I inquire what for?"

"I want to find Cassandra Boyle."

"Why?"

"Because if Thomas Boyle is hiding some family secret I'm sure she knows what it is."

"Yeah, and I'm sure she's dying to reveal it to you."

Abby told Smileowitz that Cassandra Boyle hated her brother almost as much as he did.

"But she's still a Boyle," Smileowitz reminded her. "I don't think she's going to voluntarily break rank with the rest of the gang to help us."

"Let's try finding her first," Abby suggested. "We can worry about her volunteerism later."

Smileowitz tried telling Abby that most of his investigators were busy looking into the drug dealer angle, which he thought had a lot more potential than Cassandra Boyle, but Abby wasn't easily put off.

"I'm sure you can spare one," she said. "After all, I am paying for them. Besides, I'm doing what you asked. I'm checking into the family, I have addresses for the Boyles all over the east coast, and hotels Cassandra likes in Europe. I just want someone to start checking her credit cards, or the phone company. Maybe get an idea of where she is. It's worth a shot."

"Maybe a small one. Give me what you have. I'll put somebody on it."

"SMILEOWITZ THINKS SOME pissed-off drug dealer might have killed Emily Boyle," Abby told Danny as they sat at her father's kitchen table. They were going through a stack of articles Abby had collected on the Boyles. Rain had forced their evening coffee break indoors.

"Does he actually think a dealer might have done it?" Danny asked skimming an article. "Or does he just think he can persuade a jury that a dealer might have done it?"

"I'm not sure." Abby said. "I did convince him today, though, to give me some help looking for Cassandra Boyle."

"Good for you," Danny said. Maggie was lying happily at his feet, licking his shoes. "Have you found anything in this stuff that might lead you to believe that drugs didn't have anything to do with her death?"

"Nothing concrete," Abby said. "But there is something that's bugging me."

"About the sister?" Danny asked.

"No." Abby said. "The other brother, Gilbert."

Danny looked up from the article he was reading. "Oh yeah?"

Abby told him that there was something about his death that just didn't seem quite right.

"Reporter's intuition?" Danny asked.

"It's never failed me before. Do you think you, or any of your little cop friends or relatives, could get hold of the file on the case?"

"Why? What do you think is in it?"

"I'm not sure. There's just not that much information on it in here," she patted the stack. "I thought the police reports might include a bit more detail."

"One would hope so. I assume it would be a closed file by now. I may be able to lay hands upon it, but you'll owe me."

SEVENTEEN

"ABIGAIL GARDNER, PLEASE," the deep, male voice on the phone said.

"Who's this?" Abby asked.

"Burton Lobo, ma'am. I'm a private investigator working for Howard Smileowitz. He asked me to check into the whereabouts of one Cassandra Boyle. Also requested that I keep you updated on my progress."

Abby was thrilled that Smileowitz had taken her suggestion seriously.

"The operation has not been overly fruitful as of yet," Lobo informed her.

"Terrific," Abby said.

"We do know, though, that the subject proceeded to Amsterdam, Holland via KLM flight 865 departing from Boston's Logan Airport at seventeen-hundred hours, four days ago."

"And?"

"I won't give you any false hopes, ma'am, she hasn't been seen since. No new transactions have appeared on her credit cards, and she hasn't cleared customs in any other locale, foreign or otherwise, but I'm still keeping an eye out for her."

"I appreciate that."

"Roger," he said. "I'll keep you informed of any further developments."

Since Smileowitz had banned Abby from pursuing the leads in her brother's case that actually showed promise, and Cassandra Boyle appeared to be in no imminent danger of being found, Abby went back to what she had been doing. She started her morning by re-examining everything she had found on the death of Gilbert Boyle III. Unsatisfied, she decided to try to reach Charles Delbert, the reporter who covered the story for the *News-Courier* back in 1973.

It took several calls to the paper to find out that Charles Delbert had retired in 1989. Pretending to be a lowly production assistant for "The Journal," Abby begged several staff members for his phone number. She found success only after telling a sympathetic metro editor that she was working for Maxwell Markham and that he was expecting the information when he woke up from his mid-morning nap.

Abby debated telling Charles Delbert who she was and then decided against it. Calling a reporter, retired or not, and identifying herself as Abigail Gardner, the sister of internationally-known-murder-suspect Bennett Gardner, would probably not be a good idea. Instead, she told him she was Gayle Klein of "The Journal" and then made a mental note to give Gayle a call later and warn her that she had borrowed her name.

Charlie Delbert told Abby that he remembered the story quite well. "You don't forget talking with Gilbert Boyle."

"Junior or Senior?" Abby asked.

"Senior. Junior wasn't up to talking to the press, but we couldn't shut the old man up."

"From what I've read, he seemed pretty verbose."

"I'd say," Delbert laughed. "He was screaming for blood. He wanted them to power up the chair for the guy."

Like grandfather, like grandson, Abby thought. "Do you remember much about the man who did it?"

"William Radley? Poor bastard. He was one shaken up son of a bitch. I really felt for the guy. First he kills the kid, then he has the Boyles screaming all over the place for his head. He was so petrified they could have gotten him to confess to killing the goddamn Lindbergh baby if they wanted to. If you ask me, though, he was lucky."

"Lucky?" Abby asked.

"Yeah, I did a piece once on a guy who accidentally hit Phil Correnti's kid with his car."

"Correnti, the mobster?"

"Yeah, Diamond Phil. Anyway, his kid didn't even die, but a month later the guy who hit him was found floating in Jamaica Bay. He had a pair of driving gloves stuffed down his throat."

Delightful, Abby thought. She asked Delbert what he could tell her about William Radley.

"There wasn't much to it," he said with a sigh.

"No question he was responsible?"

"It was pretty much an open and shut case. When the cops got to the scene they found him leaning over the boy blubbering like an idiot, and that was before he even knew the kid was a Boyle."

"Anything strike you as odd about the story?"

"This one? Nah, there was nothing there. If the kid's last name wasn't Boyle, the thing wouldn't have made it beyond the local papers to begin with."

Abby asked the reporter if he had followed up on what happened to Radley.

"Not really," Delbert said. "I don't remember where he was sent, but I assume he'd be out by now. I'd check with the parole guys."

"You wouldn't happen to remember where his family lived, would you?" Abby asked. "I didn't see anything on them in the stuff I've read."

Delbert thought about it for a moment. "He had a sister, I think, in the Bronx. No...maybe it was Westchester."

"Any chance you remember her name?"

"Nah, if I were you I'd get in touch with his parole officer. He would know. But honestly, I still don't understand why you're bothering with this one. I mean with the sister getting killed, I know you folks are digging deep for stories, but this one was nothing. A total zero."

"I'll take that under advisement."

After her conversation with Delbert, Abby called Gayle Klein and left a message on her voicemail warning her that she had borrowed her name. She spent the rest of her day on the phone with various officials of the Connecticut Department of Parole. It took Abby, pretending to be Gayle Klein, two hours to uncover the name of William Radley's parole officer, Arthur Dennis. It took another hour to find him and determine that Radley had finished his parole in 1988. Mr. Dennis told Abby he hadn't heard from him since.

Luckily for Abby, Mr. Dennis was a frequent viewer of "The Journal," and a member of a disconcertingly large segment of the viewing public who, for some inexplicable reason, found the work of Maxwell M. Markham fascinating. "He seems like a real good guy."

Abby thought a small fib might help. "I'm working on the story with him."

Arthur Dennis told Abby that the last address he had for Radley was at his sister's place. "But you know I can't release that information to you."

"I realize that, but I know she lives up near the Bronx somewhere," Abby said, picking one of the options Delbert gave her. "And I'm sure if you accidentally released her name and address to me, I'm sure Mr. Markham would be forever grateful."

Mr. Dennis seemed to consider this for a moment, and then he lowered his voice. "I can't give you an exact address."

"Whatever you could tell me would be extremely helpful to Mr. Markham and myself."

"Sheila Baranski," he whispered. "Mount Vernon."

EIGHTEEN

"HOW DOES A romantic evening for two in a cramped, windowless room sound to you?" Danny asked when he showed up at the Gardner household that evening.

"I'm not sure," Abby said. "I'm really more of a dinner and a movie girl myself."

"How about if the windowless room is deep within the bowels of the Milton Police department?"

"We're in?" Abby asked.

Danny smiled. "We're in."

Danny had arranged for one of Smileowitz's other *guys* to take sentry duty for him that evening. They drove to the police station in his ancient Jeep. Abby believed you could tell a lot about a person from their personal transportation. Danny's had character, but it was a complete mess. There were books, papers and CDs strewn all over the back seat. The passenger seat appeared to be used mainly as some sort of upholstered recycling bin.

The car, however, was a suite at the Four Seasons compared to the room where Abby and Danny spent their evening. Abby couldn't have cared less as she devoured the file on the death of Gilbert Boyle III.

Danny watched Abby as she read, and re-read the incident reports, and the interview transcripts concerning the case.

"Is it me," she asked. "Or is this report somewhat lacking in facts?"

"It looks kinda thin," Danny agreed.

"Thin?" Abby asked as she flipped through the crime scene photos. "The witness statements are inconclusive and the interviews are worse."

"Well, it was an open and shut case."

"You don't find this unusual?" Abby asked.

Danny thumbed through the file. "Not really. There definitely wasn't an intensive investigation involved here, but it wasn't warranted. I'll agree with you, though, that this is a little light on the facts. These guys didn't even indicate how fast they thought Radley was going when he hit the kid. That's a bit strange, don't you think?"

Abby didn't answer him. She was staring at the crime scene photos.

"Hello? Hello?" Danny said knocking on the table.

"I knew there was something funny with this."

"With what?"

"With this," Abby said as she spread the photos in front of Danny. "This is what's been bugging me about the newspaper photos."

"I didn't realize they had been troubling you."

Abby tapped the pictures on the table. "What's missing here, former law officer Morello?"

Danny looked at the pictures. "I don't know. The framing might be a little pedestrian, but I think he takes some real risks with the lighting."

"We're focusing on content only today, Danny. These are crime scene photographs from a violent accident. What's wrong with them?"

Danny concentrated on the pictures for a moment again before speaking. "The car isn't dented."

"Exactly," Abby said triumphantly.

"And the bike looks like it's in pretty good shape."

"Exactly again. This is what's been bugging me from the newspaper photos, but I couldn't put my finger on it. They all showed the same shot of a cop wheeling this thing into a police van. *Wheeling it.* If this kid was hit hard enough to cause mortal injuries don't you think the bike or the car would at least show some sort of damage?"

"You would think so," Danny said, picking up one of the pictures and examining it closely. "The car isn't even scratched."

"Shouldn't the autopsy report be part of the file?" Abby asked, shuffling through the papers.

"The paperwork might not have caught up with it," Danny offered.

"The case is almost thirty years old."

"Your point being?"

Abby asked Danny if he could get a hold of the autopsy report.

"I'm sure a copy for your personal collection can be arranged," Danny said. "But these things do not come cheap."

"Just add it to my tab." Abby knew she was onto something. She just didn't know what.

On the drive back to Easton she was so charged-up she was practically dancing in her seat.

"You're too hyper," Danny said as they walked to the back door of the Gardner house. "I'm afraid to leave you alone."

"I'm sorry," she said. "I get a little excited when a story starts to click."

"Don't be sorry. It agrees with you."

"I'm never going to get to sleep tonight."

"I can see that," he laughed.

"Want to come in and keep me company?"

WHEN ABBY LED Danny Morello upstairs to her bedroom that night, it was a first. No man or boy, outside of her immediate family, had ever made that journey with her before. She had barely touched another human being while living in her father's house. Her sixteen-plus years in her childhood boudoir were spent alone. The only sex that occurred was in her imagination. Sure, once she broke free from the house that great-great-grandfather had built, things changed. But while she was in residence in Easton, a town founded by Puritan potato farmers, Abby's physical encounters were limited to teenage passion on the front steps and an occasional aerobics video.

"I've never done this before," Abby whispered to Danny as they undressed one another.

"I don't mean to cast aspersions on your virtue," he said, "but I find that somewhat difficult to believe."

"I don't mean my first time, you idiot," she laughed. "I mean here, in this house, this room, this bed."

"Weird, huh?" Danny asked.

"A little," she said.

"Too weird?" he asked, hesitating.

"Oh no, no, no," Abby assured him. "Just weird enough to make it interesting."

Abby had to admit making love in her childhood bedroom was strange. She couldn't help thinking about her semi-invalid father sleeping downstairs, but she tried her best not to. Abby had always found sex much more of a pleasurable experience when she wasn't thinking about The Doctor.

The sex was fabulous, although Abby could have lived without Danny's suggestion that they relax post-coitally by reading out loud selections from her collection of Judy Blume books. They slept wrapped around one another that night–a position Abby normally avoided. But in her single bed they really didn't have much of a choice. Moving home as an adult was a strange enough experience. Moving home and being adult was a whole other ball game.

NINETEEN

ALTHOUGH THE POTENTIAL for a good time was certainly there, Abby's morning didn't quite work out as well as the previous evening. Things started downhill at about six when Abby realized that locking her door the night before would have been an excellent idea.

"Miss Gardner," Olga said, casting a disapproving eye towards the half-naked man sleeping beside Abby. "Your father wishes to know if you will be joining him for breakfast this morning."

Abby pulled the blanket up to her chin. "No, I won't."

"Very well," Olga clucked. "I shall let him know."

Abby hoped the declined invitation was all she would let her father know about. She could hear The Doctor speaking downstairs, but she couldn't make out what he was saying. Then she heard Olga thumping back up the stairs again. Once inside Abby's room she kept her eyes glued to the window, a scowl on her face.

"Your father wishes to know what time you will be home for dinner."

"I don't know."

"Very well." Olga turned to leave with military precision. "I shall let him know that as well."

Abby jumped out of bed and locked the door. Then she climbed back under the covers.

Danny draped an arm over Abby. "I wouldn't worry about Frau Olga. She's probably just jealous."

"Oh yeah?" Abby asked.

"Yeah. She's constantly staring at my ass. I actually find it somewhat degrading. What do you think they're having for breakfast?"

"Something non-artery-clogging. Maybe oatmeal or an egg white omelet."

"Sounds good." Danny's hands traced Abby's back and headed southward. "Maybe they'll save us a piece of toast or something."

"I wouldn't count on it."

"Did you lock the door?"

"I did."

"Too bad, we could have given Olga the thrill of her life."

"Ms. Baranski?"

"Yes."

"Sheila Baranski?"

"Yes."

Abby snuck Danny out of her bed and out of the house shortly after ten that morning. Luckily, The Doctor and Olga were nowhere to be seen. Abby showered, reheated some coffee and then got down to business. Directory assistance had only one Baranski listed in Mount Vernon, which made life very simple.

"My name is Gayle Klein," she fibbed. "I'm a producer with a television program called 'The Journal.'"

"I don't want to talk to you people."

At least she knew she had the right Baranski.

It was strange how much Abby's perceptions had changed since Bennett's arrest. She thought about the dozen members of the press who were camped out at her curb, and for the first time in her life was able to say without any trace of bull in her voice. "I completely understand what you mean."

"I highly doubt that."

"No," Abby said, "I really do, and I'd really like to talk to you about your brother."

"Yeah, I bet you would, you parasite." Abby could hear her exhaling smoke as she spoke, and was quickly forming a mental picture.

"Ms. Baranski…"

"Didn't you people get enough of us thirty years ago? What the hell do you want from us now? My brother served his time. Why can't you just leave us alone?"

"I've been looking into your brother's case and I think I've discovered something he might find interesting."

"You people are so full of crap."

"I don't think he ever hit that child," Abby said.

"What are you talking about?"

"I don't think the evidence shows he hit anyone."

"You're talking nonsense like my brother."

"I don't think it's nonsense at all, Ms Baranski." Abby was getting way ahead of herself. "As a matter of fact, I think Gilbert Boyle's death might somehow be related to his sister Emily's."

Sheila Baranski was silent, but Abby could hear her breathing on the other end of the line.

"All I want to do is talk to him," Abby said. "Would you please ask him to call me?"

"My brother doesn't need this. None of us do."

"I understand what you're saying. I truly do, but I really need to talk with him."

"Why can't you people let us forget about it?"

"Please, Ms. Baranski."

Shelia Baranski paused. Abby could hear her exhaling more smoke. "Gimme a number. If he's interested you'll hear from him."

"IT'S JUST MY GOOD name, right?" Gayle Klein asked when she returned Abby's call later that morning. "It's not my cash card or my gym membership or anything important that I have to worry about, is it?"

"You belong to a gym?" Abby asked. "I'm impressed."

"Don't be. Belonging is easy, but it does very little to help with the corpulence of my thighs."

"I hope you don't mind."

"No," Gayle said. "I'm used to my thighs. I've accepted them for the punishment from God that they are."

"I meant about borrowing your name."

"I assume this has something to do with your brother."

"That and a wire-fraud scheme I'm experimenting with."

Gayle laughed. "Excellent. Just as long as I get a cut of any profits from either of them."

"You have my word," Abby promised.

"YOU THINK HER brother's death twenty-five years ago has something to do with Emily's?" Bennett sounded as if what Abby had just told him was the stupidest thing he had ever heard.

"I didn't say it did," Abby said, trying not to sound defensive. "I just said there is something strange about it, I just don't know what."

BLOOD RELATIONS

Abby had gone to see Bennett in the prison infirmary right after she spoke with Sheila Baranski. The swelling around his face had gone down a great deal. Abby figured he must have been feeling more like his old self because he was in his evil twin personality that day. The visit was not turning out to be one of their better ones.

"So what if it's strange?" he asked. "What does it have to do with Emily's death?"

"That's what I'm trying to figure that out."

"Well, Nancy Drew, could you try to figure it out a little faster?"

"Well, Nancy Drew, could you try to figure it out a little faster?" Abby mimicked her brother in an angry, high pitched, voice the likes of which she hadn't used since she was twelve; her regression was now complete.

"What happened to Smileowitz's drug dealer fantasies?" Bennett asked, smoothing his blanket.

"He's still exploring that avenue."

"Great," he said.

Abby was in no mood for Bennett's attitude. "Listen," she told him. "If you've got any other ideas for us to look into we'd be happy hear them."

"What about space aliens or Elvis? Maybe they had something to do with it."

Abby stood up. "You know you really can be a prick sometimes. I'm trying to help you. We're all trying to help you and all we get from you are your smart-assed, snotty remarks."

Bennett didn't look at his sister. He focused instead on a loose thread on his blanket. "What do you want me to tell you?"

"Something helpful might be nice for a change."

"Like what?"

"Like anything. Like maybe someone crawled in the window after you left and killed her, or maybe she ODd and it hasn't shown up yet or maybe…"

"Or maybe she just died," Bennett said quietly, his voice catching in his throat. "Maybe it's that simple--she just died."

THE RINGING PHONE INTERRUPTED The Doctor's dinnertime performance of "Showboat." Abby went into the kitchen to answer it.

"Gayle Klein," the deep voice on the other end inquired.

"Yes." Abby craned her neck to see into the dining room. Her father seemed occupied with his dinner.

"This is William Radley."

Abby did a silent victory dance in place. "I really appreciate you calling me back."

"I have two rules," he warned.

"Yes?"

"First, I don't want to talk over the phone. You'll have to come out to Utah. That's where I live."

"That certainly won't be a problem. What's number two?"

"I want to talk to that Markham fellow."

"Also not a problem," Abby said, almost choking on the words.

As soon as Abby hung up the phone, it rang again. This time it was Smileowitz. "There's been an interesting development that I hope I won't be sorry about filling you in on."

"Why? What's going on?"

"It seems that over the past few months there have been several inquiries made about having Gwen Mason hurt."

"Really?" Abby asked.

"Ever hear of Frankie Quarters?"

"I covered part of his trial."

Two years earlier, Frankie Quarters had been tried for the execution style murders of three people in Elizabeth, New Jersey. After the killings, he allegedly chopped the victims' hands off and tossed them in the Hudson River. Quarters was acquitted after an eyewitness to the murders recanted his testimony on the witness stand.

According to Smileowitz, part of Gwen Mason's deal for getting the charges against her dropped was providing information to the police about her suppliers. "Gwen tells the cops she's getting her stuff from this guy, Peter Ganz, who it turns out is some low-level guy in Quarters' operation. Also turns out he's only slightly smarter than Gwen is."

"That's not saying much."

"The cops pick up this Ganz schmuck and he starts talking as well. The two of them start pointing fingers at Frankie."

"Smart," Abby said.

"Wait, it gets better. Genius Gwen figures that since the guy she was getting her stuff from is behind bars, all her outstanding debts are null and void."

"How much did she owe?"

"Enough."

"So Frankie put a hit out on her?"

Smileowitz laughed. "Not exactly. He wants to collect, so he has some people out looking for her."

For the first time in a month Abby felt optimistic. "This is great. Bennett's story makes total sense. He went out to pick up the food, and these guys came looking for Gwen, but they found Emily instead and killed her."

"Take a breath, Gardner," Smileowitz said. "You're getting way ahead of yourself, this is all very preliminary. You've got to stay focused on the things you've been following. I want to keep all of our options open."

"YOU FEEL LIKE going to Utah?" Abby tried to say the words as fast as possible, figuring they'd be easier to get out that way.

"Excuse me, love?" Markham said, pulling on one of his oversized earlobes. "You'll have to slow down a touch. My aural skills aren't as keen as they used to be."

Abby met Markham at The Ocean Club for coffee the following morning. At least she had coffee.

"Do you feel like taking a trip to Utah?" she repeated.

Markham put a hand across his heart. "My love, I would travel to the ends of the world for you."

"Not for me, with me."

"Even better. Any reason in particular?"

"William Radley."

"The Boyle kid killer? How did you dig that poor bastard up?"

"Legwork," she said sipping her coffee.

"Impressive, Abigail, very impressive. I know others have been looking for him. What does this have to do with me?"

"For some reason I cannot begin to fathom, he only wants to talk to you."

"A wise, wise man," Markham said. "I'll send him your regards."

"I'll give him them myself. I'm going with you."

"That might be somewhat problematic, love. If I'm not mistaken, you're temporarily suspended from active duty. I don't know if Gordo will go for it."

Abby shook her head. "I'm not going to conduct the interview, you can take Gayle as your producer and I'll go along as a production assistant or something. I looked him up because I have a few questions about the accident and I want to be there to make sure I get my answers."

"And you don't trust Maxwell Morrison Markham to do it to your satisfaction?"

"Don't be offended, but it's not your brother facing the rest of his days in jail."

"True. My brother should be out within the next two years."

"I want to go on this interview."

"I don't know, love, I don't normally like to toil with another reporter hanging over my shoulder."

"I'm the only one who knows where William Radley is."

"On the other hand, I do so enjoy your company."

"So you'll square it with Gordon?" Abby asked.

"Hmm," Markham mused, his eyes drifting. "You, me and the lovely Miss Gayle traveling together. I've had several dreams similar to this...

"Markham," Abby said snapping her fingers in front of his face. "Stay with me, please."

"I'll talk to Gordo. Consider it squared."

TWENTY

IN ORDER TO make her nine-fifteen flight to Salt Lake City, Abby had to leave for the airport by six-thirty. Her alarm clock was set to wake her at five-forty-five, but Smileowitz beat it to the punch by eight minutes.

"This Gwen thing seems to be getting more and more interesting," he said when Abby picked up the phone.

"How so?" she asked, trying to rub the sleep out of her eyes.

"Our Miss Mason seems to have disappeared."

Abby woke up quickly. "Disappeared?"

"She used her credit card in a bar at an airport in Westchester the day before yesterday. She wasn't on any commercial flight but she hasn't been seen or heard from since."

"Do you think they got her?" Abby asked, her mind racing. She didn't want to imagine what would happen to Gwen Mason if Frankie Quarters got a hold of her.

"According to my guys, not as yet, but I'll get back to you when we know more."

ABBY HAD NEVER EXPERIENCED flying with Markham prior to their journey to Utah. Being earthbound with him had always seemed like more than enough. She sensed immediately from the pair of double scotches that he ordered before their carry-on luggage was safely stored in the overhead compartment that it was going to be an interesting flight.

"He likes to learn all of the flight attendants' names," Gayle Klein warned Abby. "And he likes to use them as often as possible."

The plane was somewhat empty, so Gayle and Abby relocated to the row of seats across the aisle from Markham. He spread himself out, ordered another drink from a young woman named Betsy, and then fell asleep.

About half an hour before they were due to land, Abby made a trip to the lavatory. After using the facilities she pulled her hair back into a ponytail and donned a pair of non-prescription eyeglasses. Gayle eyed her quizzically when she returned to her seat.

"Don't be alarmed. It's just a precaution. Every once in a while I get recognized. This guy obviously watches the show and I don't want anything to screw up the interview."

"Good thinking. But I don't think you have to worry. One thing I've learned traveling with our good friend M.M. Markham over there: when he's in the room, everyone else blends in with the furniture."

Abby, Markham and Gayle were greeted at the airport by their crew, a local outfit out of Salt Lake City. "The Journal" had video crews all over the country that they hired whenever needed. The big budget network shows could afford to fly their own camera people all over the world, but most of the other programs found it more economically sound to hire locally. The typical "Journal" crew consisted of two men in their late twenties, sporting beepers, cellular phones and baseball hats. They spent a great deal of their time in a Dodge Caravan filled to the brim with video equipment, maps, and chewing gum.

William Radley's small house was on the outskirts of Park City, Utah, a forty-five-minute drive from the airport. According to what Abby was able to pry out of him over the phone, Radley had moved to Utah after he finished his parole. He worked as a truck driver for a commercial laundry.

"Mr. Radley, I presume," Markham said to the lanky, silver-haired man who answered the door.

"Mr. Markham," he said, grinning broadly. "This is a pleasure, truly a pleasure. Please come in, come in."

Abby had seen this behavior before, and it always frightened her. Untold numbers of people around the country were great admirers of Maxwell Morrison Markham. Even more disconcerting was the fact most of them were also licensed to drive automobiles and vote in open and free elections.

"I've been a huge fan of yours for years," Radley gushed as he walked them into the small living room. The furnishings were sparse, a well-worn couch, a recliner, a scratched pine cocktail table and a television set. A couple of cowboy prints decorated the walls. "I even wrote to you once while I was in prison."

Markham examined the prints. "Ah yes, the incarcerated viewing public, the most under-appreciated sector of our audience. You know a large portion of my mail comes with prisoner identification numbers on it."

"It sure is a real treat meeting you in person," Radley said. "I'm a little nervous. I've never really talked to any reporters before. Plenty called, but I knew they wouldn't believe me. I figured talking to you I'd be okay."

"I appreciate your faith in me, sir. I am confident you won't regret this."

Radley let out a deep sigh of relief. "I sure hope not."

"I'm Gayle Klein, Mr. Radley," the real Gayle Klein said extending a hand for him to shake. "We spoke on the phone. Would it be all right if we set up for the interview in here?"

"Oh, yes, yes. Wherever you wish. I'm sorry the place is so tiny."

"Nonsense," Markham said. "You have a fine, solid home here."

"Well, it's not much, but it's mine. Can I get you folks some coffee? I just made a fresh pot."

"That would be splendid," Markham said. "This is my personal assistant, Miss Abigail. Maybe she could help you with it while we start setting up."

Abby smiled at Markham and then followed Radley into his kitchen.

"I can't believe Maxwell Markham is actually here, in my house," he told Abby when they were alone. "This is very exciting, but people must tell you that all the time."

"Not all the time," Abby said glancing around the kitchen. "But just enough to cause some concern."

"I've been watching him for years. He seems like a real regular guy, you know, someone you can trust."

"I've looked into your case a bit myself, Mr. Radley."

"How does Mr. Markham like his coffee?" he asked as he poured.

"Excuse me?"

"How does Mr. Markham like his coffee? Milk? Sugar?"

"With a shot of scotch, if I'm not mistaken," Abby said. She had no idea how Markham liked his coffee.

"I don't think I have any scotch. Would bourbon be okay?"

"I'm sure the effect would be the same. Anyway, I've done a great deal of reading on the accident. I have a lot of questions about it."

"He must be a nice man to work for," Radley said as he loaded the coffee mugs onto a tray. He handed Abby the spiked one. "Why don't you take this one for Mr. Markham?"

Forty-five minutes later, the crew, under the firm hand of Gayle Klein, had rearranged the living room furniture to suit their needs. They had plugged in enough lights to illuminate a night game at Yankee Stadium, and wired both Markham and Radley for sound. The two men sat across from one another, and the camera was positioned to shoot the interview from over Markham's shoulder. Abby and Gayle took seats off to the side so as not to distract Radley. Once everyone was seated where they were supposed to be and tape was rolling, Markham jumped right in. He didn't use any of the questions or notes Abby and Gayle had prepared for him.

"My good man," Markham began. "Take me back to the summer of 1975 and tell me what you were doing with your life."

Radley nervously explained that in 1975 he was working for the U.S. Postal Service in Milton, Connecticut. He told Markham that five days a week he would travel from his small apartment in Queens, New York, to the estate-lined streets of Milton where he would sort and deliver mail to the very rich and somewhat famous.

The former mailman said he enjoyed working in Milton. He loved the pretty houses, the manicured lawns and the expensive cars. "Sometimes during my lunch hour, or on my way home from work, I would drive around town so I could look at the houses. They were all so big and beautiful. I couldn't even imagine what it would be like to live in one of them."

"Correct me if I am wrong, sir, but it was on one of these pleasure drives during the mild summer of 1975 that your path and that of young Gilbert Boyle III tragically crossed."

Radley looked at his feet. "That was a terrible, terrible day."

Markham nodded sympathetically. "Can you tell me what happened?"

"I'm not quite sure what happened," Radley said.

"Then tell me what you are sure about."

"I left work at five that day, just like I always did. And I decided to take the long way to the highway. I did that a lot in those days. I liked to drive around and look at the houses, I wouldn't bother nobody, I'd drive real slow, and I was always real careful," he shook his head at the memory and sighed. "I remember that day, I'll never forget it. I drove along Webster Avenue for a while--that was down near the beach. I took that 'til I got to Summertime Road. That's where some of my favorite houses were. Summertime is real long and twisty, so I drove real slow there, real slow. Then I made a left onto Cherryhouse Lane and I took that to Willow. That's where the accident occurred."

Abby noticed Radley's hands were shaking as he spoke.

"There's this real pretty brick house on Willow," Radley said. "It's big and has all these funny shaped windows, and it has this long driveway. I remember because I had slowed down to look at it. I just turned my head for a second or two and when I turned back I saw the boy."

"You had hit him?" Markham asked.

Radley shook his head. "No, I saw him coming towards me. He must have just come flying off the sidewalk or something, so I hit the brakes. The car sort of bucked 'cause I had slammed the pedal real hard, but it didn't really skid, it didn't even screech."

"Screech?" Markham asked.

"The tires didn't screech or anything, because I wasn't going fast."

"Then what happened?"

"Well, the car stopped. I had good brakes on that car, new ones. It was a 1967 Oldsmobile Cutlass that I had bought off a friend about a year before, and it ran fine, it ran great, but I had put in new brakes and new tires on it a couple of months after I got it. Anyway, I hit the brakes and the car stopped and then I saw the boy fall over."

"You saw the boy fall?" Abby asked before she could stop herself. All eyes turned to her.

"Thank you, Abigail, that's an excellent question," Markham said before turning back to Radley. "Now you say you saw the boy fall after the car had stopped?"

"I think so. I felt the car stop and then I looked up and I saw the boy on the bicycle right in front of the car, and then I didn't see him because he fell."

"So you don't think you hit him?" Markham asked.

Radley was shaking his head and becoming visibly upset. "Honest to God," he said, placing his hand over his heart. "I don't believe I hit that child. I stopped in time."

Markham nodded his head. "Then how do you explain the boy's injuries and his death?"

"I don't know. I can't explain what happened to that boy. I wish I could, but I can't. I remember after the accident racing out of the car to see if I could help him. He was just lying there. He looked like he was sleeping. He wasn't bleeding or anything. I tried to wake him up, but I couldn't, so I ran to the nearest house and told them to call the police. I've spent years thinking about that poor child, thinking about what happened that day, and all I know is that I didn't hit him, I didn't. I don't know what hurt him so bad that he died, but I really don't think it was me."

"You went to jail for a substantial amount of time for this, didn't you?"

"Ten years," Radley said.

"You pled guilty to manslaughter?"

"Yes, sir, I did, but I had no choice."

"What do you mean you had no choice?"

"This little boy was Senator Boyle's son. The poor man had just lost his wife a few years before and now this. They told me if I didn't plead guilty there would be a trial and that no one would believe my word over the Boyles. They said that they would get me for murder and then I'd be put away for maybe the rest of my days."

"Who told you this?" Markham asked.

"Gilbert Boyle."

"The Senator?"

"No, his father," Radley said. "He came to see me in jail with a couple of his lawyer friends and the man from the district attorney's office. They told me if I said I did it, they would talk to the judge for me personally and that I would be out in ten years. I may not be a math genius or anything, but ten years sounded a lot better to me than the rest of my life."

"Did you have a lawyer?"

"I had one of them legal aid lawyers. He told me that the whole country loved the Boyles, and if we went to trial I would lose. He kept saying 'take the plea, take the plea.'"

"We've looked at the photographs that the police took of the crime scene," Markham informed him. "The pictures that were taken of your car at the scene didn't show any damage. Did you see your car after the accident?"

"I didn't look at my car. I was trying to help that little boy."

"Then you didn't see any damage to your car?"

"No, they took me away pretty quick. But if I didn't hit anyone why would there be any damage?"

"What about the bike?" Markham asked.

"I didn't pay much attention to that, either."

Markham asked Radley about his years in prison, and then they discussed what he'd been doing since he got out. After he was sure that he'd covered everything, he asked Gayle and Abby if they had any other questions.

Abby pounced immediately. "How can you be sure that you didn't hit him with your car?"

Radley looked at Markham. "I guess I can't be, but I got to go with what I believe. I spent ten years in prison thinking about that day, the worst day of my life. I've replayed those few seconds in my head over and over and over again, and I swear to you, that little boy is always on the bike when the car stops."

"Are you positive?" Abby asked.

William Radley looked her straight in the eye. "Yes, I am."

TWENTY-ONE

GAYLE KLEIN AND Maxwell Markham returned to New York a couple of very happy television people. Abby knew promos of "Boyle Killer Speaks" were dancing through their heads. Abby came back from Utah somewhat less jubilant and much more confused.

"If Radley swears he didn't hit Gilbert Boyle, his car wasn't damaged, and the kid's bike still looked brand new, then why did that boy die that day?"

"That's an excellent question," Danny said as he watched Abby skip stone after stone into the Long Island Sound.

"Thanks, I've been asking myself for hours."

Danny removed some papers from his back pocket and unfolded them. "Well, maybe you can find some of the answers in this."

"What's that?"

"The medical examiner's report on Gilbert Boyle III."

Danny hadn't gotten the word "report" out of his mouth before Abby had snatched the papers away from him.

Abby tried to read the papers by the moonlight. "What does it say?"

Danny shook her head. "I'm not exactly sure. I think it's in Latin or something."

"Great," Abby said trying to skim the report. "We need to get someone to translate this for us."

"It's too late tonight to find someone," Danny said. "You'll have to wait until tomorrow."

Abby started for the house. "Want to bet?"

"Dad," Abby whispered, gently touching her father's arm. "Dad, wake up, I need to ask you a question."

It was ten-fifteen, and the lights in The Doctor's room were still on. Maggie, who was sleeping at the foot of the bed, began growling as soon as she sensed Abby's presence. The noise didn't disturb The Doctor however; he was lying in bed with his eyes closed, an open book face down on his chest. As soon as Maggie saw Danny she stopped growling and started thumping her large tail against the bed. Unfortunately, that didn't wake The Doctor either.

In most cases when in pursuit of a story Abby wouldn't think twice about stomping her feet or dropping something acoustically significant on the floor to rouse the target of her interest, but when the sleeping person is both a recovering stroke victim and her father, it becomes a much more complex issue. She decided to wake him anyway, reasoning that since this concerned Bennett, The Doctor would have an interest. Also, maybe if he stayed up a bit later at night, he would let her sleep a little later in the morning.

"Dad," she said, squeezing his arm harder.

"Huh?" The Doctor said snapping out of a sound sleep. It took him a moment to focus. "Abigail, what's wrong?"

"I'm sorry to wake you," Abby said with a lifetime's worth of reluctance, "but I need your help with something."

THE DOCTOR USED HIS STRONG hand to flip the pages of the report. "Interesting, very interesting."

It was the only thing he had said besides "hmm" in the five minutes since Abby handed him the autopsy report.

Abby wasn't good at waiting. "What's in there that's so interesting?"

The Doctor continued reading. "Practically nothing. That's what makes it so interesting. This basically says that he died from internal bleeding brought on by massive trauma. He bled to death."

"That much we knew." Abby was amazed by how much her father's speech had improved in the weeks since his stroke.

"It also says there weren't any bruises on the body. Just a couple of scrapes from where he hit the pavement."

Abby found that interesting. "No bruises?"

"Nothing major."

"Emily Boyle didn't have any bruises on her either," Abby reminded all present.

Danny wasn't impressed. "So, they're not a family of big bruisers. Maybe they all took iron supplements. Emily Boyle wasn't hit by a car."

"No, according to the police, she was hit by my brother. Besides, according to William Radley, Gilbert Boyle wasn't hit by a car either."

Danny shrugged. "What are the odds? A convicted killer who says he didn't do anything."

"You didn't speak with the man," Abby reminded him. "I did."

"May I interrupt with my opinion?" The Doctor asked.

"Sorry, dad. What do you think it means?"

"I'm not sure it means anything. This report is somewhat cursory. It may be just a coincidence."

"Well, what if it's not a coincidence?" Abby asked.

The Doctor used his good hand to scratch his head. "They could have died too quickly for bruises to form. That's one possibility. There might be some sort of heredity factor that results in a lack of bruising. But if so, it only means neither of them bruises. What is the connection with their deaths?"

"If you take into account that Bennett says he never touched Emily, and William Radley says he never hit the kid, then do you think the lack of bruises is irrelevant?"

"I don't know, Abigail," The Doctor said. "You wanted a translation, not an expert witness. Post-mortems are not my area of expertise. In this case, I think it might be more judicious for you to get a second opinion."

"I WOULDN'T WORRY about it right now," Smileowitz said as he stirred his coffee and reviewed his morning agenda.

Abby had been waiting for him when he arrived at his office shortly after seven. "What do you mean you wouldn't worry about it right now?" she asked.

Smileowitz looked up from his desk. "Which part didn't you understand?"

Abby was dumbfounded. "The whole thing. I think we should get someone else to go over the autopsy report. I think there might be a connection between the two deaths. At the very least it's worth looking into."

"I'll tell you what I think is worth looking into," Smileowitz said. "The tropical paradise known as Barbados."

"You're going on vacation?"

"Not exactly. I think we've found the bewitchingly disturbed Gwendolyn Mason."

"In Barbados?"

"It seems Gwen's father caught her performance on 'The Report' a couple of weeks ago."

Abby smiled. "That must have been a proud moment for him."

"I have it on good authority that he was disgusted, but even more important, he was embarrassed. Lawton Mason doesn't like bad publicity, especially when it's generated by his offspring, so he paid off her debts..."

"Lawton Mason paid off Frankie Quarters?"

"Cash with interest. Then he had Gwen shipped off to his place in Barbados to dry out. She took his private jet. That's why there was no trace of the flight. I'm going to head down there today to try and see her."

Abby rolled her eyes. "I'm sure she'll be dying to talk to you. She's real fond of Bennett."

"Yeah, well, it's called exculpatory evidence and we have a right to it. That's what they have subpoenas for."

"How about if I go with you?"

Smileowitz grinned. "You don't know how much I'd love to spend a couple of days in some tropical paradise with you and a big bottle of coconut oil, but you're not getting anywhere near this witness. Maybe after this shit is all over, though, the two of us will zip down there for a naughty little weekend."

"Sorry," Abby said, as a frightening image of Smileowitz in a small Speedo bathing suit flashed though her mind. "The offer's only good during trial preparation."

"Dammit."

Abby asked if he'd heard anything further about Cassandra.

"No, and I wouldn't pin too many hopes on that one. I'll check on it today, though, and have Burt Lobo call you later."

"Great," Abby said without enthusiasm.

"Keep going with that autopsy thing, though, that sounds interesting."

"Interesting?"

"Hey, I'm not ruling anything out. Why don't you play around with that one a bit and see where the shit lands? At least it will keep you busy while I'm dealing with Ms. Mason."

Abby left Smileowitz's office that day feeling even more dejected and useless than she had before. She was an experienced investigative journalist, and the thought of following up leads just for the sake of keeping busy was insulting. She knew if Smileowitz thought that her theory had any merit at all he'd have thrown her off of it and let one of his *guys* look into it. Abby tried to drown her misery with an extra-large, double-shot latte. Then she went to see her brother.

"THE IDEA THAT GWEN Mason might have had something to do with this doesn't exactly shock me," she said. Abby's hyper-caffeinated blood had her doing laps around the visitor's room. "Smileowitz is really into it, too."

Bennett rubbed his chin. He had been released from the infirmary that morning. "I don't know. I just don't buy it."

"Why not?" Abby asked.

"If someone was looking to hurt Gwen, why would they kill Emily?"

"You want to examine the reasoning behind a mob-drug hit?"

"What about the thing you were looking into, the guy in Utah?" Bennett asked.

Abby wasn't as excited about it as she had been. "There's definitely something not right there, but I'm not sure what it has to do with your case."

Bennett looked confused. "Not right where?"

He listened intently as Abby explained about the autopsy reports and what William Radley had to say.

"Well, as far as theories go, Smileowitz seems to have simplicity and plausibility on his side," he told her. "But yours definitely gets points for originality."

"I'VE GOT SOME good news and some bad news," Burt Lobo told Abby when he reached her at her father's house later that afternoon.

"Take your pick, Burt," Abby told him.

"Well, we found Cassandra Boyle's hide-out in Amsterdam."

"Great."

"Unfortunately, she left there yesterday."

"Where did she go?"

Lobo paused. "We're still trying to ascertain that, ma'am."

"I don't understand what's so difficult about it," she asked. "Doesn't she use a passport like the rest of us, or is she able to leap over customs agents in a single bound?"

"It isn't that simple."

"Obviously not."

"May I speak freely, ma'am?"

"Please. I didn't realize you were holding back."

"The regular rules don't apply with these folks. They're Boyles. They're not like everyone else."

WITH NOTHING ELSE to occupy her energies, Abby decided to take her father's advice on the autopsy report, and seek another opinion. She didn't want just any opinion; she wanted the best. She called Felix Weitzman.

It seemed like a lifetime ago that Abby interviewed Dr. Weitzman in Washington. She hadn't thought about her beloved AIDS dentist piece in a while.

It took a couple of hours and several phone calls to reach the good doctor, but he sounded happy to hear from her.

"Ms. Gardner!" the heavily accented voice on the other end of the phone said. "How are you doing?"

"I've been better."

"Yes, I had heard that your difficulties multiplied since we last spoke. Until I spoke with Mr. Burrows in your office, I did not connect your name to the Boyle murder. How is your father holding up with all this?"

"He's doing well. Thanks for asking."

Abby told Dr. Weitzman why she was calling. She explained to him what she knew about the deaths of both Emily and Gilbert Boyle III. Except for a couple of "uh huh" or "ahs" he let her do most of the talking.

"The thing that keeps nagging at me is the lack of bruises. Both of them died in violent situations, one supposedly from a beating, and the other after being hit by a car. And neither one has any significant bruising. I thought that was odd and I wanted to see what you thought about it."

"Do you have the post-mortems on the Boyles?" he asked.

"I have the brother's, but I can get Emily's."

"Good. Fax them to me, then we'll talk."

ABBY SHARED A QUIET dinner with her father that night. He questioned her about how Bennett was doing and she told him about Dr. Weitzman. Then they played gin rummy, sang "My Fair Lady" and watched television until The Doctor fell asleep.

Howard Smileowitz's Caribbean trip was the talk of all the news programs that night. All of the shows aired the same blurry photograph of him deplaning at the Barbados airport. They all turned speculation on what he was doing there into several minutes of airtime. The guesses ran the gamut from a mystery witness to plastic surgery.

"The Journal" mentioned Smileowitz's trip south, but devoted most of their show to the second part of their story on William Radley. "The Report" had an interview with another alleged old friend of Bennett's that Abby had never heard of. This one, Chuck Grasso, claimed to have painted houses with Bennett a few years before. Grasso's real contribution to the program, though, was a home video of Bennett and a lot of other people at a beach party. Bennett, running around with a beer in his hand, and wearing just a pair of shorts, appeared quite inebriated. He spent the majority of his on-camera time gnawing on the ears of two young women who seemed rather fond of both Bennett and each other.

"He sure had a way with the ladies," Grasso told the viewing audience in his burn-out monotone. "They couldn't get enough of him. I think he might have been into guys, too, but you know, whatever, we had a great time together. We were wasted constantly. Half the time we'd leave the windows closed when we were working cause the paint fumes helped extend the buzz."

"Late Edition" featured an interview with former golden boy Campbell Dawson. He wanted to explain to the world about his past misdeeds, but said he couldn't under the advice of counsel. He did want to tell everyone about his forthcoming book.

"It's a tribute to Emily--warts and all--and I think she really would have liked it. The eight pages of color photographs that will be featured in it were some of her personal favorites."

ABBY WATCHED TELEVISION until midnight, and then went upstairs to nap until Danny finished work at two.

As far as regular disruptions of her sleep patterns went, Abby much preferred Danny's late night visits to Gordon's early morning phone calls. She discovered that the strangeness of making love in her father's house had ebbed a bit with practice. Danny was the one person who could take Abby's mind off her brother, if only in brief spurts.

Once they were resting in the afterglow, Abby told Danny all about Smileowitz's theory. "There is one thing that bothers me though," she said.

"Which is?"

136

"There was no sign of forced entry at Emily's place. I can't imagine she would open the door to some drug-dealing hit man."

Danny propped himself up on an elbow. "Maybe she knew the guy. Maybe he got a key at some point from Gwen."

"I suppose that's possible, but there was no sign of a struggle. I mean, Emily Boyle was not exactly the timid, reserved type. I don't think she would have just sat there and let this guy beat her to death. She would have gone down kicking and screaming, which brings us right back to the bruises again. This guy didn't leave a mark on her? It doesn't make any sense."

Danny pushed Abby's hair out of her face. "It doesn't have to make sense. It's not Smileowitz's job to convict someone else for the crime. All he has to do is establish reasonable doubt in the mind of one juror and your brother is a free man."

Abby knew he was right.

TWENTY-TWO

"I'VE GONE OVER the reports that you sent me several times," Dr. Weitzman said when he telephoned Abby the next morning. "I know it's ghoulish, but I must admit I find this all terribly interesting. I feel like Quincy."

Abby told the doctor that she really appreciated him taking the time to help her.

"I assume that by your asking me for my opinion that you obviously don't subscribe to the authorities' hypothesis on the Boyle siblings' deaths?"

"I have some problems with their theory," Abby said as she stirred milk and sweetener into her second cup of coffee that morning. "In their version of events my brother is a murderer."

"Well, that's understandable. But unfortunately for your brother, their theory has some credence."

"Two siblings die in unrelated, allegedly violent deaths years apart, both without any bruises on their bodies. I mean if it was only one of them, maybe, but both of them? Doesn't that strike you as a little odd?"

"So would it be correct to presume that you're bypassing coincidence and leaning towards some sort of familial predilection for unnatural deaths?"

"I'm not leaning anywhere," she said, sipping her coffee. "I'm just trying to help my brother."

"Very well, then," Weitzman said. "We are confronted with quite an interesting scenario here. Someone dies of traumatic injuries without evidence of a violent demise. No lacerations, no edema, no contusions and no external bruising. Yet, in both cases, death is attributed to massive internal hemorrhage as a result of physical trauma. Now, keep in mind that my background is not pathology. I am an internist with a specialization in hematology, which is the study of diseases of the blood or blood-forming tissues. Your hunch of a familial condition that can produce the findings described in these reports can be corroborated by medical literature."

Abby grabbed a notepad and pen off the kitchen counter. "So it *is* possible that something else caused their deaths?"

"The question is not so much possibility as it is plausibility. Almost anything is possible, but here it is plausible that they died either directly of some other condition, or were just prone to suffer extensive internal hemorrhage from extremely minor trauma."

"What?" Abby asked. She was already lost.

"It is possible that they bled to death from what appear to be minor injuries. But it seems more plausible that there is something else going on here."

"Such as?"

"Such as a blood condition that would cause an affected individual to bleed to death from a physical force so slight that it would barely bruise the average person. Something like bumping your head on a low-hanging shelf or walking into a wall."

Abby was surprised. "Someone could die from that?"

"There are several blood disorders that if you were predisposed to, a minor bruise could be fatal. But you know at this point all we're talking about is speculation and theory. The information in the reports you sent me is far too limited for me to even begin to make any sort of a diagnosis."

"I'm not looking for a diagnosis," she assured him. "Just some direction."

"That, I can help you with. Now, the differential diagnosis is quite extensive and includes various platelet disorders, vasculopothies, acquired and inherited coagulopothies..."

"Hold on, Doc," Abby laughed. "My last science class was eleventh grade chemistry."

"Maybe we should start out with some basic blood physiology."

"Good idea."

"Your body forms blood clots in order to prevent uncontrollable hemorrhaging or bleeding, to patch up, if you will, a damaged blood vessel. Sort of how you might repair an automobile tire. This is a complex process that requires a host of factors which must act in concert. Basically, a blood clot is formed by the actions of the damaged blood vessel, platelets and various plasma factors."

Abby started taking notes. "What's a platelet?"

"A platelet is a cellular fragment that is found both lining the blood vessels and free-floating in the bloodstream. They contain a number of compounds that direct clot formation and affect blood flow."

"Okay," she said. She was with him so far.

"Now, conditions that affect any one of these three arms of the clotting process, the blood vessels, platelets, or plasma factors, can result in a bleeding disorder. I'm sure you're familiar with hemophilia."

"Yes." That one she'd heard of.

"Hemophiliacs either lack or are deficient in a plasma factor involved in clot production. However, almost all individuals who suffer from hemophilia are male."

"What else is there?"

"Well, there's Von Wollebrand's disease, which affects platelet function and causes reduced plasma factors. This condition is noted for increased bruising, bleeding from the gums and heavy menstrual flow."

"Well, wouldn't the lack of heavy bruising rule that one out?"

"Yes, it would, but I'm just throwing things out here. There's also a group of conditions known as collagen vascular diseases that can result in blood vessel injury. I'm sure you've heard of Lupus, which is one such condition."

"Yes."

"Now, with these disorders, once they reach the severe stage, there is almost always evidence of damage to other organ systems, such as the lungs or the kidneys. This is true of a host of other conditions that affect platelets as well."

Abby could hear Dr. Weitzman shuffling papers on the other end of the phone.

"There's also something called Osler-Rendu-Weber syndrome or Hereditary Hemorrhagic Telangiecstasia."

"What's that?"

"Well, this condition, which is usually referred to as HHT, results in abnormal blood vessel formation. Affected individuals suffer from excessive nosebleeds and have lesions in the gut and lungs, from which they may suffer massive hemorrhage. This particular disorder is obviously hereditary and affects both men and women equally."

"How exactly would you know if you had any of these things?"

"Well, with most of them you could tell with a blood test, but with HHT, besides the characteristic bleeding history, you need to check for lesions on the skin, the brain and the lungs."

"Ick."

"There are also various nutritional disorders and some exceptionally rare heritable disorders that can result in excessive bleeding, but they are perhaps less likely."

Dr. Weitzman spent the next forty minutes rattling off diseases and disorders at lightning speed as Abby tried to take it all down.

ABBY COULDN'T SLEEP that night, and eventually gave up trying. Her conversation with Dr. Weitzman earlier that day had provided her with a bevy of information, but still no answers. Shortly after midnight she sat down at the desk in her bedroom and started reviewing her notes. She went over and over the list of exotic sounding ailments Dr. Weitzman had told her about. She kept reading, hoping something would make sense. She must have stared at it for close to an hour before it hit her.

"Of course," she said to no one in particular while underlining Osler-Rendu-Weber syndrome. "*Of course!*"

In parenthesis next to the strange sounding illness she had scribbled the words Hereditary Hemorrhagic Telangiectasias, aka HHT.

"HHT." Abby repeated to herself as she searched for the notes she'd taken from Emily Boyle's purloined medical files. "HHT" Abby sang as she raced through what she had written until she found what she was looking for.

"Has inherited her mother's HAT."

Bennett's words echoed through Abby's head: "Maybe, she just died."

TWENTY-THREE

"**WHY WOULD A DOCTOR** make a note about someone's hat in their medical file?" Abby asked Danny breathlessly.

She had leapt over a sleeping Maggie and sprinted downstairs to share her discovery with Danny. She found him patrolling the backyard.

"I don't know," Danny said. "Maybe the guy had some sort of head gear fetish."

"I must have read it wrong," Abby insisted. "It must have said HHT, not HAT."

"Considering the average doctor's penmanship it might have said 'rhododendron.' We've got to get a hold of that file again."

"You're right," Abby said. "We need to find Markham now."

Danny looked at his watch. "It's almost two o'clock in the morning."

"Great, then he's probably still at The Ocean Club. At this hour I can make it there in forty minutes."

"Why don't you just call him?" Danny suggested.

"Can't," Abby said, shaking her head. "At this time of night if you don't have direct eye contact with Markham, any conversation you have with him is useless."

"You want a ride? I'm off in fifteen minutes."

"That would be great."

"It's completely self-serving. The last time I went somewhere with you I got lucky."

MAXWELL MORRISON MARKHAM was exactly where Abby said he would be. It was forty-five minutes before The Ocean Club shut down for the night, and he was holding court at the end of the bar. Always keeping one eye peeled for women entering the place, Markham spotted Abby as soon as she walked in.

"Young Abigail!" he bellowed across the bar. "What a delightful surprise!"

"Geez," Danny whispered to Abby. "I've heard about this guy."

Abby took his hand and walked towards the bar. "Prepare to be amazed. Either that, or repulsed."

After Abby made the introductions, Markham stood to shake Danny's hand. "My good man, I truly hope you appreciate the depth of your good fortune when it comes to female companionship. Abigail here is a lovely, lovely, nubile lass whom I admire with every fiber of my being."

"Danny works with Smileowitz," Abby told Markham.

"Are you a lawyer or organized crime figure?"

"At the moment, neither."

"He does security work."

"I see. Then might I surmise from your late appearance here and the presence of your gendarme that this is not a social call?"

"I need to see that medical file again."

"Why?"

"Because I'm curious about Emily's rubella vaccinations," Abby said, crossing her arms. "I need to check something in it."

"Now, now, my dear, you are going to have to get markedly more specific, and somewhat less snotty, if you expect me to attempt to procure that file again. What is it that has rekindled your interest in it?"

"I can't tell you that. I just need you to do this for me."

"Abigail," Markham purred.

"Look, I can't have this all over the news tomorrow, Markham, it's too important."

"Oh, now I'm intrigued. How about if I swear to embargo the information until you tell me I can employ it?"

"How about if I swear that you'll be the first to know anything once we figure this out? Please?"

Markham seemed to ponder this for a moment. Either that or he dozed off, Abby wasn't sure.

"I really do need your help with this," Abby said, forcing herself to touch Markham's arm. "And, I promise you, if this pans out, it will be worth it. I just need to get hold of that file again."

"All right, love. For you and an exclusive, I'll see what I can do."

"WHAT IF THE question isn't who killed Emily Boyle, but *what*?"

"Explain this to me again," Smileowitz said.

"What if there was a rare underlying medical condition that caused Emily Boyle's death, something that made it look like she had been assaulted?"

"That part I got. Go over the rare medical condition again."

Abby had reached Howard Smileowitz in Barbados by phone a few hours later. For once she got to wake him.

"It's called Osler-Weber-Rendu syndrome or Hereditary Hemorrhagic Telangiectasias." Abby said.

"Teleke-what?" he asked.

"It's also known as HHT. Weitzman described it as this hereditary disorder in which the blood vessels form abnormally. There is some kind of short circuit or something in the circulatory system that makes it so that even a minor trauma, like bumping your head or walking into a wall can lead to massive blood loss."

"And you think Emily Boyle had this Hereditary Hemorrhagic whatever?"

"Not just Emily. I think her brother Gilbert and her mother had it, too."

Smileowitz sounded doubtful. "And this is because her medical records mentioned a hat?"

"I thought it said *hat* when I read it the first time, but now I realize that it must have said *HHT*."

"Well, we need to get a look at those records again."

"Markham's working on that now."

"Okay, so explain to me how this works."

"Dr. Weitzman told me that people who have it usually have these lesions that look like purple spiders on their skin, and that they're also found internally on the GI tract, the lungs and the brain. The lesions signify the short circuit, and a lot of the time the people have nosebleeds or bleeding in the GI tract to go along with them. According to Weitzman, in people who suffer from HHT, extreme physical violence would not be necessary to produce a major internal injury. Moderate physical force could lead to a lesion giving way and a major bleeding episode. So when Bennett says that all he did was push her away he could be telling the truth. If she suffered from HHT, the impact from the push might have been enough to kill her. In any case, it would explain the lack of bruises and the way she died."

"That's a pretty big if," Smileowitz pointed out.

144

"Well, it would also explain William Radley's version of events. Just falling off the bicycle could have killed Gilbert Boyle III if he had the disease."

"It's a possibility."

"It's more than a possibility," Abby insisted. "I saw her medical records. This thing was in there. I just didn't know what it was at the time."

"Just try not to get too crazy with this yet," Smileowitz told her. "I'm going to talk to Gwen Mason today and I'll be back in New York first thing tomorrow. Between now and then, Markham should be able to get hold of those records. Let's start with those, and your brother. See what he knows. Then between that and Ms. Mason we'll figure out how to proceed."

"DREADFUL NEWS, ABIGAIL my love," Markham said when he called that afternoon. "The file is gone. My associate went back to re-filch it and someone had beaten him to it."

"Damnit," Abby said, shaking her head.

"This is not a pleasant turn of events. I stayed true to his regulations. No copies were made of that document and this is the thanks I get for it."

"There's got to be something that we can do," Abby said.

"I'm exploring several other avenues. But, if I were you, I'd talk to Smileowitz about what legal options you have to procure the medical documents."

BURT LOBO CALLED right after Abby spoke with Markham. His news wasn't any better. Cassandra Boyle had arrived in Madrid, Spain, the previous day, but hadn't been seen since.

"She didn't check into a hotel?" Abby asked. "Board another flight?"

"Not as far as we can tell," Lobo told her. "But we're working on it."

ABBY MET SMILEOWITZ FOR breakfast the next morning to talk about the missing medical file.

"The records may not necessarily be gone," he said between forkfuls of scrambled eggs. "They just may have been moved."

"Great. Now we've got a conspiracy on our hands."

"I'm not saying it's a conspiracy," he said, pointing at her with his fork. "But I think it's worth looking into. I want to talk to this Dr. Weitzman, and then I want to talk to your brother."

"Why? What happened to Gwen Mason and her murderous drug dealer?"

"They are still alive and doing well." Smileowitz glanced around the restaurant to make sure no one was listening and then lowered his voice. "I had lunch with Gwen yesterday. After her fourth gin and tonic, she confirmed for me that she owed money to her dealer and that people were looking for her."

Abby was thrilled. "That's great, that backs up your theory."

"Just keep it tucked under your hat, Gardner. Right now, it's probably our best bet, but we still need to check out every possible lead."

TWENTY-FOUR

"Hereditary Hemorrhagic what?" Bennett Gardner asked.

"I find it a lot easier just calling it HHT," Smileowitz told him.

"Do you remember Emily ever saying anything about it?" Abby asked.

Bennett shook his head. "Not that I recall."

Abby and Smileowitz had gone to visit Bennett right after Smileowitz had spoken by telephone with Dr. Weitzman. Weitzman had told Smileowitz that he needed further information on Emily before he could attempt a diagnosis, but he felt that if a history of HHT was actually mentioned in her medical records that he would take that as a very strong indication that she suffered from it.

"Did Emily ever have nosebleeds?" Abby had given Bennett the short version of the dissertation she was putting together on HHT.

"Not that I can remember."

Smileowitz took a seat across from Bennett. "But you weren't around her twenty-four hours a day."

"That would be correct," Bennett said. "We did spend a few moments apart."

"And you had only known her for a year?"

"Yes, and during that year I never saw her nose bleed. However, I did see it run once. Of course she was suffering from a cold at the time," Bennett said, smiling at his lawyer. "What happened to your killer drug dealer fantasies?"

"I wouldn't be doing my job if I didn't run down every possibility."

Abby sat down next to her brother. "Did you ever notice any purple lesions on Emily's body?"

"Purple lesions?"

"Yeah. Small ones that look like spiders. They're a sign of HHT."

"Small purple spiders?"

"Small purple spiders," Abby repeated.

Bennett thought about it for a moment. "You know, she did have a couple of little marks on her hips, but she said they were birthmarks or stretch marks or something."

Smileowitz leaned back in his chair and fondled his ponytail. "I think I'm gonna call Tony Warner at the D.A.'s office. He's a pretty good guy. I'm thinking I might want to throw this one out at him and see how he reacts."

Abby looked at Smileowitz. "You don't think the district attorney knows about it, do you?"

"No, I'm sure they don't. By law, the prosecution has to turn over all exculpatory evidence to the defense. Warner would be flirting with disbarment if he didn't. Thomas Boyle, though. Now that's another story."

"Wouldn't that be an obstruction of justice?" Abby asked.

"Amongst other things," Smileowitz said.

"You really think he'd do that?" Bennett was dumbfounded.

Abby looked at her brother. "In a political heartbeat."

Smileowitz stood up. "Depending on what Tony says, I may move to subpoena Emily's medical records this afternoon. I'm also going to get in touch with Burt Lobo, and have him put a few more people on this Cassandra thing."

"Really?" Abby smiled. "That sounds like an excellent idea."

ABBY HAD DINNER with her father, who peppered her nonstop with questions about Bennett and Dr. Weitzman. Mercifully, his stream of consciousness inquiries were cut short by the telephone. Abby raced to answer it.

"Abigail?" the voice on the other end oozed.

"Yes?"

"It's your uncle, Stan."

Her skin began to crawl. "What do you want?"

"It's always a pleasure to hear your voice as well, my dear niece."

"What do you want?" she repeated.

"I had a rather strange visit from Thomas Boyle today."

"What was so strange about it?"

"Well, normally he hates my guts and does everything possible to avoid me," he said.

Maybe Boyle had a redeeming quality after all, Abby thought to herself. "What did he want?"

"He wanted my mother's recipe for apple brown betty. What do you think he wanted?"

"I don't know," Abby said. "Let me think. He was coming to see you...perhaps he wanted advice on how to divert more federal money to tobacco farmers by eliminating school lunches for disabled children. Or maybe he was trying to figure out the best way to propose a tax credit for people who join country clubs."

"I didn't want to eliminate the lunches Abigail. I just didn't know why they had to have hot ones everyday."

"What did Boyle want?" Abby demanded.

"Well, it seems the poor man is still under the erroneous assumption that I have some sort of influence over you and your brother."

"He wants you to convince Bennett to take the deal?"

"You're a very perceptive young woman, Abigail. You remind me of your mother."

"What did you tell him?"

"I told him that although I thought the deal was an excellent idea, I was unfortunately no longer actively involved in my nephew's defense."

"Good."

"He intimated that it might be in my best interest to become actively involved, especially where the plea bargain is concerned. Apparently, Thomas really wants this to go away."

"And you told him?"

"I told him that I don't appreciate threats. Then he mentioned something about campaign financing, mail fraud and the problems associated with running for re-election as felon."

"What a prick."

"Truthfully, I think Thomas Boyle gives the rest of us pricks a bad name. In any case, the little putz left my office in a full-blown huff. I just thought you and your present counsel should know that he contacted me."

"Thanks for letting me know," Abby said.

"I'm just trying to help."

"Don't ruin the moment by spreading bullshit all over it, Stan."

"Good God, you really do remind me of your mother."

EACH DAY SINCE SHE had moved back in with her father, Abby waited to see who would be the one to prevent her from sleeping past six-fifteen in the morning. Smileowitz and Olga, operating as her father's proxy, had been running neck and neck in the early riser's derby, but Smileowitz's phone call at five-thirty that morning pushed him out in front of the pack.

Abby picked up the phone and then pulled the blanket over her head.

"Good morning," Smileowitz bellowed.

"Isn't it a little too early for you to be in a good mood?"

"I got a call from Anthony Warner, assistant district attorney last night."

"Really? I got a call from my uncle last night."

"My condolences," Smileowitz said. "What did he want?"

"Thomas Boyle stopped by to see him yesterday."

"What a coincidence, he and Warner want to see us later today."

Abby moved the blanket from her face. "What do they want?"

"I imagine it has something to do with the subpoena. Now the fun should really begin."

"WE'RE A LITTLE curious about the subpoena and the motion for the Brady hearing," A.D.A. Anthony Warner said as he rolled a pen between his thumb and forefinger.

"I'd imagine you would be," Howard Smileowitz told him.

Abby and Smileowitz were seated in a law-book-lined conference room in the Sussex County District Attorney's office. Across a large faux-oak table sat Warner and Thomas Boyle.

Before the meeting, Smileowitz had elicited a promise from Abby that she would let him do the talking. It was either that, he said, or he would lock her in the car. Abby got the feeling from the way Thomas Boyle was sitting silently and glaring at her that Warner had struck a similar deal with him.

"I'm ninety-nine percent sure we're going to try to quash the subpoena," Warner said. "But I wanted to give you the opportunity to try and talk me out of it. You might be able to if you explain what you're looking for."

Smileowitz nodded in Thomas' direction. "I think you might want to talk to Mr. Boyle here about that. I'm sure he knows exactly what we're after."

Warner sat back in his seat. "I don't think that's the best idea right now. He's a little upset over this, you know, digging through his dead sister's past to try and save her killer's neck. Very nasty business."

"Alleged killer," Smileowitz reminded him. "And we're not digging through her entire past, just her medical records."

"The truth is, even if I wanted to turn over the records to you I probably couldn't," Warner said.

"Is that so?" Smileowitz asked, his face betraying nothing.

Warner shifted in his seat. "We seem to be having some trouble locating them."

Abby couldn't help herself. "How convenient."

Smileowitz shot her a silencing glare. "They're missing?"

"We're not sure," Warner said.

"They're more than missing," Thomas Boyle hissed. "They were stolen and I want to know where they are."

"Mr. Boyle, please," the prosecutor said. "We don't know that."

"Where did you get your information about the medical records, Ms. Gardner?" Boyle demanded.

"I hope you're not implying that I know where the records are," Abby said.

Smileowitz put a hand on Abby's arm. "Gardner..."

Boyle sneered at Abby. "Oh, please. I know what you do for a living. I know the sleaze that you work for. You parasites pull crap like this all the time, and I'm tired of it. I want to know where you got your information. Who did you buy it from?"

"Actually, Tommy," Smileowitz interrupted, "according to our experts, we don't necessarily need your sister's medical records to find out what we need to know. Apparently, your mother's or your brother's would do just as well. You know what?" he said patting himself down for a pen. "That's a good idea. Let me make a note to file for another subpoena."

"Listen to me, you scumbag," Boyle said, pointing a finger at Smileowitz. "If you think I'm going to stand by while you attempt to clear your client's name by dragging my family through the dirt, you're out of your mind."

Smileowitz stood up. "Go to it, Tommy. Abby, I think we're finished here."

Boyle stood up. "Your brother is going to fry, Ms. Gardner. Then I'm going to come after you and your lawyer."

"I suppose this means you're definitely going to move to quash the subpoena?" Smileowitz asked Anthony Warner as he held the door open for Abby.

"Count on it," Boyle said.

SMILEOWITZ WAS GRINNING as he drove Abby home. "Oh boy is he pissed off. And something tells me it's not about the disappearing records."

"Maybe he was just having a bad morning."

Smileowitz laughed. "He was definitely having a bad morning, and you, me, and whatever's in those medical records are a big part of it. Poor Tony, he has no idea what's going on."

"You're not starting to agree with me are you, Smileowitz?"

"I don't know, Gardner. I wasn't too sure about it before, but after seeing Lord Thomas' reaction in there I'm beginning to think we may be on to something here."

"We really need to find Cassandra," Abby pointed out.

"I wouldn't count on locating her. Now that Thomas knows what we're after, he's going to personally make her disappear,"

"Great. Then what's our next step?"

"We've got to wait for them to schedule the hearing."

"Super," she muttered. Some things never change.

TWENTY-FIVE

"JUST KEEP YOUR mouth shut and don't fucking move."

Abby was awakened that night by the unpleasant sensation of cold steel pressed against her throat. She opened her eyes to see a man wearing a ski mask looming over her. She could hear Maggie growling outside the door.

"What do you want?" Abby asked, trying not to sound petrified.

The man grabbed the phone line and ripped it out of the wall. "I told you to keep your mouth shut."

She decided to do as she was told.

"Get the fuck up," he said, pulling her to her feet and slamming her hard against the wall. The noise made Maggie bark. "You better listen, and listen good."

Abby closed her eyes and bit her lip. Where the hell was Danny?

"You tell that lawyer of yours to stop asking so many fucking questions. If he keeps sticking his fucking neck in where it doesn't belong, it's gonna get chopped off."

Abby couldn't help herself. "You mean his nose, don't you?"

"What?"

"You mean chop his nose off, not his neck."

"Shut the fuck up," he said bouncing her against the wall again. Abby could hear Maggie jumping up on the door and growling. The force of the large Labrador trying to propel herself through the door made the wall shake, which seemed to make the man nervous. Abby began to reconsider her relationship with the dog.

"Let's make this simple," the man hissed. "You better stop fucking around and convince your brother to take that fucking deal.

That coke-head bitch got exactly what she deserved and if someone is going to pay for it, it better be him. You know what I mean? So you better tell that lawyer of yours to back the fuck off, and stay the fuck out of any of them stupid fucking island nations, or the next time I come to see you I'm going to stop in your daddy's room first." He ran the knife along her cheek. "Then you and I will have some real fun."

He shoved Abby face down on the floor and told her to count to one thousand before getting up. Then he climbed out the window. Abby could hear Maggie scrambling down the stairs and out the back door.

Never being one to follow rules, Abby only made it to thirty before belly-crawling out of the room and bolting downstairs to the kitchen phone. She dialed 911 and then ran outside to look for Danny.

She found him lying face down near the shrubs along the side of the house.

"Oh God," Abby said, kneeling down beside him.

Once again, sirens could be heard wailing in the distance.

"I REALLY THINK YOU should let us take you to the hospital," the police detective said.

"I'm not going anywhere," Danny insisted from his supine position on the living room couch. He had regained consciousness before the paramedics even had their equipment out of the rescue.

"I think you should go and let them check you out," Smileowitz echoed. He had arrived shortly after the police.

"I'm fine," Danny said. "I actually enjoy a little chloroform every once in a while."

"Did you see anything?" The Detective asked.

"Nothing, the guy came up behind me."

Neither Danny nor Abby was able to give the police much of a description of the late night intruder. The only one who was able to provide any helpful information at all turned out to be Maggie. She returned home just after the police arrived, panting furiously, and clutching in her teeth fabric torn from the seat of the masked man's pants, as well as what appeared to be a small piece of his ass.

After she handed over the evidence to the police she gulped water from the downstairs toilet bowl for a few minutes and then collapsed at Abby's feet.

"I assume he came in the window," Abby told Smileowitz, Danny and the police. "Since that's the way he left."

Smileowitz nodded at Abby. "How's your neck?"

"It's fine," she said, touching the shallow cut the knife had made. "He barely broke the skin."

"You're lucky that's all you got." Smileowitz said.

"Believe me, this guy wasn't intending to kill me. He just wanted to frighten me."

"And all he said was that Bennett should take the deal?" the defense attorney asked.

"No, he also told me that the coke-head bitch, I believe those were his exact words, got what she deserved, and that you shouldn't stick your neck in where it doesn't belongs or it might get cut off."

Smileowitz thought about it for a second. "Wouldn't that be my nose?" he asked.

"That's what I said, but he didn't seem to appreciate me correcting his clichés. I think that's why he drew blood."

"No one likes a smart ass, Gardner."

"He also mentioned something about he'd prefer it if you would stay away from those *island nations.*"

Smileowitz smoothed his hair. "You know, this guy sounds like he's trying awfully hard to convince us that he's working for that unknown, possibly homicidal drug dealer we're looking for."

Abby nodded. "I was thinking the same thing."

Smileowitz looked at the cut on her neck. "This guy wasn't working for some drug lord, that's for sure. You wouldn't still be here if he was."

"So who do you think sent him?"

"I'll give you one guess."

ABBY FINISHED WITH Smileowitz and the police around two, and then spent another hour watching her father's breathing after she told him what happened. Then she went back to sleep.

She, of course, was awakened several hours later by Smileowitz, who showed up at the house accompanied by an alarm company technician. He promised security-wise he would take the Gardner household into the twenty-first century by later that afternoon. Smileowitz wanted every window and door in the place wired. The Doctor was all for it.

"I am so very sorry," The Doctor kept repeating. "I should have done this years ago. Then maybe I could have prevented everything you went through last night."

Abby was a little sore from the previous evening's activities, but she kept telling her father she was fine and not to worry. Truthfully, though, if he was going to explore modern household technology she would have preferred cable TV. She figured if she was going to spend a good portion of her time sitting around doing nothing, she might as well do it with HBO and Showtime.

"I spoke with Lobo this morning," Smileowitz told Abby as they watched the technician alarm the windows.

"Have they found Cassandra?"

"No," he said, shaking his head. "She seems to have vanished."

SMILEOWITZ STAYED AND had breakfast with The Doctor and Abby. Together they watched the morning news and did a few numbers from *Fiddler On The Roof*. The programs all attempted to cover the break in at the Gardner house, but since the police had released few details besides the sketchy fact that whatever had happened involved Abby, most of them stuck with showing footage of the rapidly growing press assemblage in front of the house.

"Geez," Abby said, surveying the crowd on TV and out the window. "You would think with that many people around someone might have noticed a guy in a ski mask rappelling down the side of the house."

The network morning shows didn't have much more to offer than their local counterparts, except for their ability to let the entire nation in on their lack of information. Not easily discouraged, they all trotted out their legal talking heads who joined in the speculation about what went on in Abigail Gardner's bedroom the night before.

After breakfast, Smileowitz told Abby that he was meeting with the D.A. and the judge later that day about the medical records. "Your presence is not required. You can stay here and rest."

"I'm fine. I'd rather go to the meeting."

"Sorry, no relatives. The judge only wants lawyers. I get the feeling she doesn't want to have to deal with Thomas Boyle, either."

"Oh, c'mon," Abby said.

"Invitation only, baby," Smileowitz said shaking his head. "I'm going to try and settle this today, but I don't think it's going to happen."

"Boyle's never going to hand over that stuff without a fight. He's got too much riding on it."

"I doubt if there's anything left to hand over."

Once Smileowitz had gone, Abby convinced her father to continue with his normal morning therapy routine. Then she fell asleep on the living room couch.

An hour later she was roused from her nap by yet another ringing phone.

"What the hell happened last night, love?" Gordon Burrows asked, trying to sound concerned. "Are you jealous of all the attention your brother is getting?"

"Yes, Gordon, that's exactly it. I was feeling neglected and unloved so I hired some ape with a knife to climb in my window and rough me up a bit."

"Are you all right?" he asked.

"I'm fine."

"Glad to hear it. I had a rather strange phone call this morning."

"Oh yeah?"

"Actually, Roger Wilkes at 'The Report' had the strange phone call. Then he rang me to share it."

"What was so strange?"

"Roger said he got a call at home late last night from a man who claimed to be a private investigator. He said he had information on you and your questionable journalistic practices."

Abby was amused. "Someone called Roger Wilkes to talk about *my* questionable journalistic practices?"

"Roger found it pretty ironic as well."

"What did they say?" Abby laughed. "That I was sleeping with my sources, or paying them in cash and drugs?"

"All of the above, which of course only served to get him interested in hiring you away from us. But they also mentioned something about your mental health."

"Such as?"

"That you've been under the care of a psychiatrist since your mother was killed."

"I wish," Abby said. "I'd be a far better adjusted adult if I was. And probably in the midst of one of those healthy relationships I keep hearing so much about."

"He also said that you ran away from home when you were sixteen."

"I went to college."

"And then he mentioned the tantalizing little tidbit that you had been institutionalized several times during the last ten years for drug and alcohol abuse. He told Roger the last time was about a year ago."

Abby was flabbergasted. "And he offered proof of this?"

"No, Roger never let it get that far. He knew it was bullshit."

"I didn't realize I was so well respected by my peers."

Gordon laughed. "Yes, well, I'm sure you are, love, but Roger said he knew it was a load of crap because if you were working for a fat rat bastard like me, there was no possible way you had the time to fart, let alone be institutionalized."

"He knows you well."

"Yeah, but unfortunately, not everyone else does. Trust me. Someone will take this guy up on his offer."

TWENTY-SIX

"YOU BETTER MAKE sure you get enough sleep tonight. You're taking the stand tomorrow."

Smileowitz called Abby at about three in the afternoon.

"I gather the meeting didn't go well?"

"About as well as expected. But if you really want to ruin your afternoon, turn on the television," he said.

"Why?" Abby said, reaching for the remote.

"Boyle is holding another press conference."

"Great." Abby flipped channels until she found him orating from the steps of the Sussex County courthouse.

"Well, you might as well watch what he has to say, and then meet me down at the jail. I want to talk to you and your brother about tomorrow."

Abby hung up the phone and then raised the volume on the TV. She didn't want to miss a word of what Boyle had to say.

"It is the shame of our justice system that it is not structured to protect the victim," Boyle said angrily. "I am a part of this system and I think it is something we need to change. Tomorrow, Bennett Gardner and his attorney will go into court to demand Emily's personal medical records so they can rummage through her brief life history for something, anything, that they can use to confuse a jury, to make them think that somehow this was her fault. Well I am here to tell you that I will not stand idly by and watch it happen. I loved Emily too much to allow them to pick through her ashes in order to find something to trash her with. I will not let them do that to my sister."

HOWARD SMILEOWITZ was in full-court prep-mode as he strode the now familiar length of the Sussex County Jail's visitor room. "Dr.

Weitzman is flying up tomorrow morning. He's going to go first, then Bennett, then you."

Bennett was still having trouble believing what his attorney and sister were telling him. "I just don't get it. If Emily really had this HHT thing, why wouldn't Thomas just say so? Why wouldn't he or Cassandra or someone else just say that's what happened? Why would they put me through all this?"

"Because he's an asshole," Abby said.

"That part I know, but I can't believe they knowingly sent that other guy away for ten years."

Abby was losing patience with her brother. "You just don't get it, do you? To them he didn't matter, you don't matter. When Emily's brother died her father was talking about running for president. Grandpa Boyle wasn't going to let anything get in the way of that--let alone the truth."

"But what difference does it make?" Bennett asked

"It makes all the difference," she insisted. "Their image is everything. They didn't want the world to know about this thing that they have, this weakness that runs in the family. They're supposed to be perfect people, the ideal that everyone wanted to be, the family that everyone would vote for. They must have figured if the general public thought Gilbert Jr. had some mysterious disease that could kill him if he tripped over the rug in the oval office he'd never get elected. Him or any other Boyle. It was easier to send William Radley to jail for a decade than admit what really killed that kid. Besides, you've got to figure that the sympathy vote is worth a couple of percentage points."

"And you both think that's what they're doing now?" Bennett asked.

Abby threw up her hands.

"Look, Bennett," Smileowitz said, pulling up a chair. "If they came right out and admitted it at this point, Thomas Boyle's political career would be destroyed. They'd have to reveal that they knowingly sent an innocent man to jail for ten years and they tried to do worse to you. Boyle gets a lot better press if he's the grieving brother of a crime victim, not the brother of some former druggie who bled to death from an obscure blood disorder."

Bennett shook his head. "He gets better publicity if Emily's a murder victim."

"Yes," Abby said.

Smileowitz told Bennett that he'd probably need him to testify about the lesions he'd seen on Emily's body. "I really don't want to have to call you because then they can question you."

"Let them question me," Bennett said. "I have nothing to hide."

"Good," Smileowitz said, patting Bennett's arm. "Now with your sister here, we may have some other problems."

Abby crossed her arms and looked at both of them. "Such as?"

"Such as when you testify about seeing HHT in Emily's medical records, I'm sure Warner is going to want to know how the hell you came to be looking at those medical records."

"Tough," Abby said.

Smileowitz shook his head. "I got the feeling that would be your answer. Tomorrow won't be dull, boys and girls. That I guarantee."

TWENTY-SEVEN

"WHAT IS HE doing here?" Abby whispered to Smileowitz as they entered Judge Gower's courtroom on the fourth floor of the Sussex County Justice Center.

The "he" Abby was referring to was James Chandler. Chandler was midway through his third term as the Sussex County district attorney.

"My guess is that Tommy-boy didn't like the way the case was being handled," Smileowitz said. "I got the feeling Warner wasn't inclined to fight the subpoena."

"Really?"

"Yeah, but something tells me his inclinations were overruled."

Anthony Warner was already seated at the prosecutor's table, looking miserable. Chandler was huddled nearby with Thomas Boyle. Boyle glared at Abby and Smileowitz as they walked into the courtroom.

They glared right back.

THE MORNING HAD begun well. Burt Lobo had called first thing to report that Cassandra Boyle had arrived in New York that morning on the red-eye from San Francisco. How she had gotten to San Francisco wasn't exactly clear, but he had it on good authority that she had landed at Kennedy Airport at six-thirty-five A.M. Smileowitz had people fanning out to all corners of the northeast to check known Boyle addresses and hangouts.

"OSLER-RENDU-WEBER syndrome, which is also known as Hereditary Hemorrhagic Telangiectasia, or HHT, is a hereditary disease of vascular malformation or abnormal blood vessel formation. It affects both women and men and, as its name suggests, is passed on from parent to child."

Felix Weitzman, MD, was the first witness Smileowitz called. The bow-tied Dr. Weitzman appeared every inch the authoritative scientist as he explained the disorder to the court.

"Diagnosis of HHT is made on physical examination. Laboratory studies of those suffering from the condition are usually normal, except for evidence of iron-deficiency anemia which is found in most patients."

Smileowitz stood in front of the defense table, pen and legal pad in hand. "How is it diagnosed then?"

"The disease is noted by the presence of small purple telangiectatic or spider-like lesions on the face, body, oral and or nasal mucosa and the tips of the fingers and toes. Lesions may also be found throughout the mucosa of the GI tract, the lungs and in the brain. When these lesions rupture they can result in major episodes of bleeding."

"It sounds dangerous."

"It is," Dr. Weitzman said.

Weitzman explained there was no preventative treatment for HHT. Doctors could only treat the symptoms.

"Most patients," he explained, "require continuous iron therapy to replace the iron that is lost because of the constant mucosal bleeding."

"Doctor, do you have any opinion as to what caused the death of Emily Boyle?"

"From the information I have, I am unable to make a diagnosis. But after studying the autopsy reports on both Ms. Emily Boyle and her brother, I am confident in saying HHT is a possible cause of death. At the very least it certainly warrants further investigation."

"Thank you, doctor. I have nothing further."

James Chandler stepped up to the plate. His tone was brusque and his cross-examination to the point. "Sir, have you ever met or examined the victim in this case, Emily Boyle?"

"No, I have not."

"And the information that you've made your diagnosis from was obtained from where?"

"I haven't made a diagnosis. I have only offered my opinion as to a possible cause of death."

"And in forming that opinion you got your information from where?"

"From the autopsy reports on Ms. Boyle and her brother."

"Have you spoken with any of the police detectives who investigated this case?" Chandler asked.

"No, sir, I have not."

"Did you read any of the police reports on the case?"

"No, I did not."

"So you didn't have any information regarding where the body was found, the condition it was in, the crime scene itself or any other evidence that the police gathered?"

"No, I did not."

Chandler was incredulous. "But in your opinion, Ms. Boyle's death can be attributed to a rare hereditary blood disorder?"

Weitzman calmly explained that he believed HHT to be a possible cause of Emily's death.

"But you cannot say conclusively that this disorder caused her death, can you?"

"No," the doctor admitted, "I cannot."

THE NEXT WITNESS Smileowitz called was Bennett. He had been allowed to forgo his bright orange prison jumpsuit for the hearing and took the stand dressed in a baggy blue suit.

The night before, Smileowitz had gone over the questions he would be asking him. He told him he would only ask three, and warned him to keep his answers short and to the point. "The idea is to get the information we need out, without leaving them much to cross-examine you about."

"Did you ever notice any lesions on Emily Boyle's body?" Smileowitz asked.

"Yes."

"Can you describe them for the court?"

"Objection!" Chandler jumped to his feet. "Your Honor, this is irrelevant, not to mention morbid."

"Overruled." The judge instructed Bennett to answer the question.

"Emily had several small purple spider-shaped marks on her hips and her stomach. She told me they were stretch marks."

"Did you ever see Emily take iron supplements?"

"Yes."

"Thank you. I have nothing further."

"HOW WOULD YOU DESCRIBE your relationship with Emily Boyle?" James Chandler asked Bennett on cross.

Smileowitz stood up. "Objection, Your Honor."

Each question Chandler attempted to ask Bennett was greeted with an objection by Howard Smileowitz. Eventually, Smileowitz remained standing, rather than jumping up every twenty seconds to register an objection. The only thing James Chandler was able to establish was that Bennett did indeed have enough personal knowledge of Emily Boyle to know where any birthmarks she had might be.

AFTER A RECESS for lunch, the hearing resumed. Smileowitz's next witness was Dr. Alicia Keene, the Sussex County medical examiner. She performed the autopsy on Emily Boyle.

Dr. Keene testified that Emily's death was the result of a massive cerebral hemorrhage brought on by suspected trauma.

Smileowitz looked at her quizzically. "Suspected trauma?"

"I determined that trauma was the most likely cause of her injuries."

"And what was the basis for your suspicion?"

"A number of factors. The police report, the bleeding."

"But 'suspected trauma?' you're not one hundred percent convinced?"

"No, not one hundred percent," Dr. Keene said.

Dr. Keene testified that the bruising she found on Emily Boyle's body was minimal.

"Now, suppose you didn't have the police report. Would you still suspect major trauma?"

Chandler shot to his feet. "Objection, Your Honor, the witness is not here to rewrite the autopsy report."

"It goes to our theory on how the death occurred, Your Honor." Smileowitz argued.

"I'll allow it," the judge said.

"Doctor, if you discounted the police account of what they claim happened would you still suspect a major trauma caused the cerebral hemorrhage that killed Emily Boyle?"

"I might look for other causes for the bleeding."

"Would one of those other causes be a blood disorder, something along the lines of HHT?"

"Yes," Dr. Keene allowed. "A blood disorder might be a possibility."

"Thank you, doctor. I have no further questions."

As soon as Smileowitz was done with his questioning, Chandler was on his feet. "During the course of your examination of Emily Boyle, did you see any lesions on her body that would lead you to suspect Hereditary Hemorrhagic Telangiectasia, or any other blood disorder of that type?"

"No," she said shaking her head. "I did not."

"Thank you," Chandler said, smiling. "I have nothing further, Your Honor."

On re-direct Smileowitz asked Dr. Keene if, during the autopsy, she had been looking for the lesions normally associated with HHT. She said she had not.

"Is that something that you would normally look for when conducting an autopsy on the victim of an assault?" Smileowitz asked.

"No."

"Is it possible they were there and you just didn't see them?"

Chandler jumped to his feet, but the judge overruled his objection.

"Yes," Dr. Keene answered, "it's possible the lesions were there and I just didn't see them."

SMILEOWITZ'S FINAL witness of the day was Abby.

"Several weeks ago, did you have the opportunity to read the medical file of Emily Boyle?"

"Yes, I did," Abby told the court.

"And how did that opportunity come about?"

"I was given the file by a confidential source. I was allowed one hour to read it."

Chandler stood to object. "'A confidential source,' Your Honor?"

"You'll have your turn on cross, Mr. Chandler," the judge said.

Smileowitz nodded at Abby. "Ms. Gardner, can you tell the court if you read anything in Emily Boyle's medical file concerning the blood disorder known as HHT?"

Chandler jumped up again. "Objection, Your Honor, this witness is not a doctor. She is not qualified to testify about a medical file."

"I'm not asking her medical opinion, Your Honor. I'm only asking her about what she read."

"I'll allow it, Mr. Chandler. The witness will please answer the question."

Abby was happy to oblige the judge. "There was a notation in the file that said that Emily Boyle had inherited her mother's HHT."

"WHAT DO YOU DO for a living, Ms. Gardner?" Chandler inquired on cross-examination.

"I am a journalist."

"Are you currently employed?"

"I work for a television program called 'The Journal.'"

"You are currently suspended from your job as a, uh, journalist, aren't you?"

Abby didn't like the way Chandler said "journalist." It was okay, though, because she was certain he wouldn't like the way she said "lawyer." She told the court she was on a temporary leave of absence.

Chandler could barely hide is contempt as he asked Abby to explain how she came to see what she believed was Emily Boyle's confidential medical file.

"I was offered it by a source."

"And you are positive that this was indeed Emily Boyle's medical file?"

"Yes, I am."

"Is it possible that this was a fake file?"

"I don't believe so. Other information in the file has been verified."

"Who was the person who showed you the file?"

"It was shown to me by a confidential source."

"Ms. Gardner, you expect us to believe that you saw the file, and that you read HHT in the file, but yet you won't tell us how you came to see the file?"

"I told you it was confidential."

"Are you aware of the fact that the file is missing?"

Abby glanced at Smileowitz. He shrugged. "No, sir, I am not."

"Emily Boyle's medical records were kept in the Smithfield, New Jersey, office of the late Doctor William Fenton's associate, Dr. Milton Reynolds. They were taken in a burglary two weeks ago, along with the medical records Dr. Fenton kept on the rest of the

Boyle family. Would you happen to know anything about that, Ms. Gardner?"

"No, I do not." Abby could see Smileowitz scribbling on a legal pad. She was sure he was thinking the same thing she was: that all of the records were gone. Every piece of paper that ever contained the name Boyle and any mention of a blood disorder was more than likely part of a smoldering ash pile by now.

"Do you think your confidential source might know anything about the burglary?" Chandler asked.

"I don't think so," Abby said.

Chandler again demanded that Abby tell him who gave her the file and again she refused to answer. The district attorney then turned to the judge and requested that she direct Abby to answer the question.

"Objection, Your Honor," Smileowitz said, standing up. "Ms. Gardner is a journalist. Her sources are privileged."

"But she's not testifying here as a journalist," Chandler insisted. "And, in fact, she wasn't working as a journalist when she saw the file."

Smileowitz didn't buy Chandler's argument. "What does that have to do with anything? She is still a journalist, whether she's on a leave of absence, on vacation or taking a sick day."

"Your Honor, the defense is asking the court to believe this woman's testimony about what she read in a confidential medical record that has since been stolen. I think if we are expected to believe that these records truly mentioned this mysterious disease, then the state must first be permitted to ascertain that what Ms. Gardner claims she saw were actually Emily Boyle's medical records. In order to do this, we need to know how she came to see these records to begin with. The identity of the source that showed her the file is directly related to the credibility of the testimony."

The judge agreed and ordered Abby to answer the question. Abby told her she couldn't.

Judge Gower didn't look happy. "You can't or you won't?"

"I refuse to answer the question," Abby said.

"You do realize that if you refuse to I will have to hold you in contempt of court."

"Yes, I do."

Judge Gower looked at her watch. "Considering the late hour I think we should recess now for today. Ms. Gardner, I advise you to use this evening to reconsider your answer. We will resume here tomorrow morning at nine-thirty, at which time you will either answer the question or be in contempt of this court."

BY THE TIME Abby and Smileowitz had said goodbye to Bennett and made their way to the front steps of the courthouse, the press had been fully informed about Abby's testimony and the legal dilemma she was facing.

"Abby!" they called as she and Smileowitz pushed their way through the crowd. "Did you steal those records? Are you really going to go to jail over this?"

Abby tried to ignore the press swarm as they trailed them to Smileowitz's waiting car. "Are you really going to choose your source over your brother?" someone shouted.

"I am not choosing my source over my brother," Abby snapped as she struggled to open the car door.

Smileowitz urged her through gritted teeth to stay quiet and get in the car. The reporters pressed on.

"Abby! Thomas Boyle claims you're attacking the victim," one of them shouted.

"We are not attacking Emily," Abby said. "We are looking for information on her blood vessels. We think she suffered from an inherited medical condition that Thomas Boyle knows all about, and it's *that* condition that killed her, *not* my brother. Boyle won't tell the truth, though, and we can't find his sister Cassandra to see if she'll help us. We have no choice. We need the medical records to give us the answers the Boyles won't. My brother loved Emily. He wouldn't have hurt her for the world."

TWENTY-EIGHT

"Abigail, my brave little lamb. There is no need for this. I will gladly take the punishment for you."

Maxwell Markham was waiting with The Doctor and Danny when Abby and Smileowitz returned from court.

"Don't worry about it," Abby insisted. "I can handle it."

Smileowitz sided with Markham. "Why don't you just give him to Gower? He'd enjoy the time away and then we could keep you out here on the outside where you're needed."

"I'm not telling her about Markham or anyone else," Abby said. "It's a matter of principle."

"Principles, schminciples, love," Markham argued. "It's my source, I should be the one imprisoned for it."

"I'm reasonably confident there are several reasons why you should be behind bars," Abby told him. "But this isn't one of them."

"Abigail, please." Markham pleaded. "You are needed here. Your father needs you, your brother needs you."

"My brother is already in jail, maybe we can have lunch together on the inside."

Smileowitz agreed with Markham. Abby ignored both of them and turned to Danny. "Will you stay here with my father if this really happens?"

"No problem, as long as your father is okay with it."

Abby looked at her father.

"Just do what you have to do, Abigail," The Doctor said. "I'll be fine."

Danny Morello ran a finger down Abby's bare back. "I've never slept with a condemned woman before. You're practically insatiable."

Abby laughed. "I'm not condemned, I'm contemptible."

"You're really killing my buzz here, you know."

Abby's date with the department of corrections was delayed for a day while The Law Network cable channel led the charge of media outlets filing a motion, asking for the right to televise the rest of Bennett Gardner's evidentiary hearing. She put her stay of incarceration to good use and spent the early part of the morning in bed with Danny.

She spent the later part of the morning hounding Howard Smileowitz and Burton Lobo for information. The Cassandra Watch had entered its second day, and was still far from fruitful. The youngest Boyle had not surfaced in any of the locations Smileowitz's people were watching. Her phone number showed no activity, her credit cards had not been used, and her checking account remained untouched.

AFTER A FULL day of legal arguments, Judge Gower opted to let the camera in the courtroom.

OVER BREAKFAST THE following morning, Abby's father assured her that he'd be fine at the house without her. "What's one more child behind bars?"

"I'm really sorry about this," she told him.

"You have nothing to be sorry about. You're doing the right thing, Abigail, and you've been doing it all along. You've taken good care of your brother and your old man and I'm proud of you."

"Really?"

"Really. Now finish your breakfast. Who knows what they'll feed you in the big house."

ABBY AND SMILEOWITZ were escorted into the Justice Center the following morning through a rear door. In order to avoid the press and the general public, they were sent upstairs in the lumbering freight elevator. Unfortunately, they had the bad luck to share it with Thomas Boyle and James Chandler.

"You had to do this the hard way, didn't you?" Thomas Boyle hissed as soon as the elevator doors closed. "You couldn't have convinced your client to take the deal, Howie? After he gets convicted he's going to sue your ass for malpractice."

"My client happens to be innocent, Tommy," Smileowitz informed him. "And if I can convince a judge to give me a search warrant for your house and your office, I'm sure I can find the medical files to prove it."

Boyle's face turned crimson. "What the hell does that mean?"

Smileowitz smiled at him. "It's called obstruction of justice. Unless of course you're even more stupid than I think you are and you destroyed the file. Then it's called something entirely different."

"Are you accusing me of having something to do with the disappearance of those files?" Boyle took a step towards Smileowitz. "Is that what you are saying?"

"Gentlemen, please." James Chandler stepped between them. "Let's keep this discussion friendly."

Smileowitz smoothed his hair. "You know something, Tommy? I hope those files really are gone because then I'll have reason to ask the court to dig up your mother and your brother. Then we'll find out what really happened, unless of course, they get misplaced, too."

"You are an asshole!" Boyle shouted, lunging for Smileowitz. Chandler placed a hand on his chest to hold him back. "When this is over, I'm going to have you disbarred."

"Exactly how much does disbarment cost these days?" Smileowitz wondered out loud.

Abby laughed.

"You know what, Tommy-boy?" Smileowitz said as Boyle's face turned even redder. "Your having fucked with those files is probably the best thing you could have done for my client. I'll have to tell him to send you a card after he gets out."

AT PRECISELY NINE-THIRTY, Judge Gower resumed the hearing. Abby was again asked to take the stand and was reminded by the judge that she was still under oath. James Chandler then asked her one more time to name the source that provided her with Emily Boyle's medical records, and again Abby refused.

"Your Honor," Chandler said, glaring at Abby. "Would you please direct the witness to answer the question?"

Smileowitz stood up. "Judge, I want to object to this once again. Ms. Gardner is a working journalist, and protecting her sources is part of her job."

"And directing the witness to answer the question is part of my job," Gower said. "The witness will answer the question."

Abby refused.

"Very well then, Ms. Gardner, you leave me no choice. You are in contempt of this court. You will be held in the county jail until this matter is resolved. I will have you brought back to this court tomorrow morning to see if you have changed your mind. Officers, please take the witness into custody."

TWENTY-NINE

ABBY'S NEW HOME was a ten-foot-by-ten-foot cell located in a separate area of the Sussex County Jail from the general population. Her only company was a rotund, balding guard in his late fifties named Jerry, whose desk was stationed a few yards from her cell. Jerry seemed to be a pretty cheery fellow considering his line of work. He informed Abby he had worked for the county for twenty-seven years and was a huge Maxwell Markham fan.

"That Markham," he laughed, shaking his head. "He seems like a hell of a guy."

"That he is."

"Any chance he'll come by while you're in here?"

"That's actually the true beauty of Markham," she said. "You just never know."

JERRY WAS KIND enough to turn on his small portable television so he and Abby could watch the five o'clock news together. The day's events in the Emily Boyle murder case were the top three stories. News of Abby's imprisonment led, followed by Thomas Boyle's utterances for the day. Abby thought he did a pretty decent job of pretending to avoid the press and their barrage of questions as they chased him down the courthouse steps.

"What do you think of today's developments? How did you feel in court, Thomas?" they shouted. For a moment it appeared that for the first time in his life, Thomas Boyle might actually decline comment. But after a short parking lot pursuit he finally gave in to his natural urges and spoke.

"I am angry," Boyle told the horde. "I am angry about what happened in there. Today was a painful exercise in confusion orchestrated by the defense. Bennett Gardner, his family and his attorney are trying to confuse the issue by creating a spectacle. It was devastating to watch, but it pales compared to what the defendant's lawyer told me before we got into court this morning. Howard Smileowitz promised me that if the files don't turn up he is planning on asking the court to exhume the bodies of my mother and my little brother, Gilbert." Boyle's voice cracked effectively when he spoke about his family. "After Emily was murdered, I didn't believe that things could get much worse, but I was wrong. Now these people are going to attempt to dig up my mother who died almost thirty years ago, and my little brother who was killed twenty-five years ago, and for what? To defend the man who murdered my sister. Their indecency goes beyond my comprehension and I will not allow them to defile the memory and the remains of my family in order to make some grotesque play at distracting a jury. I will fight them every step of the way for my sister, Emily, and my mother and my brother."

Boyle actually had tears in his eyes when he finished. Abby thought it was a brilliant performance, but it didn't end there. The third story of the evening featured a packed press conference Boyle held later that afternoon from a shelter for battered women in The Bronx.

"My sister Emily didn't like the spotlight," he told the crowd. "Unlike her big brother she hid from the public eye. But I believe she'd be happy with what we are here to do today. Domestic violence kills thousands of women each year in the United States. It's an ugly statistic that was made much more real to me and my family with the loss of Emily at the hands of her boyfriend. My sister's murder has attracted an unprecedented amount of media attention, and it is my hope that some good will come from that. If only one woman somewhere finds the strength to walk away from a bad situation, then my sister will not have died in vain. It is with this hope that I am pleased to present this check for two-hundred-and-fifty-thousand dollars from the Boyle family trust to the Women's Project of New York. This group runs four shelters for women and children in The Bronx and Queens and assists battered spouses with the legal help they need to make sure they don't become a victim of the courts as well. We are donating this money in memory of Emily with the hope that it will help prevent other senseless murders like hers."

"GOWER WANTS TO hold off on a ruling in order to see what you're going to do," Smileowitz told Abby when he visited her that evening.

"I'm sure Boyle is thrilled."

"I'm sure he is."

Abby asked Smileowitz if he'd gone by to check on her father yet. She had elicited a firm promise from him that he'd look in on The Doctor while she was in jail.

"Stopped by after court. I wanted to explain to him how I managed to get both of his kids incarcerated."

"Is he alright?"

"He's fine. I had to convince him not to go out to yell at the parasites on your front lawn, though. He wanted to show them your journalism degree."

"Super."

"Ready to feel worse?"

"I'm always ready to feel worse."

"Cassandra Boyle went through customs in Paris this morning."

Abby's heart sank. "Great, now what do we do?"

"Well, unless you're planning on heading into court tomorrow morning to reveal your source, we wait."

"Even if I gave the judge Markham's name, it won't do any good. I don't know who the hell he got the file from, and I am sure he's not going to tell her. We would still be stuck with the same problem, only we'd have the additional thrill of watching weeks and weeks worth of stories based on Maxwell Markham's prison diary."

ABBY WAS BROUGHT into court at ten o'clock the following morning. At eleven, the judge again asked her to reveal the name of her source, and again Abby refused. By noon she was back in her cell.

Jerry was on duty that night, too, and together they watched the news. Reporters were starting to ask a lot more questions about HHT. Experts from several major medical centers were interviewed about the blood disorder, and various high-ranking Boyles declined comment.

Abby was positive Thomas Boyle would not be happy about the media's newly-aroused interest in HHT and the curious medical history of his family. But she knew the added attention could only help her brother's case. She hoped that it would only be a matter of time before some other journalist uncovered another definitive connection between the Boyles and the deadly blood disorder.

THIRTY

THE FOLLOWING MORNING, Abby was dressed and ready for court by eight-thirty. When ten o'clock rolled around and still no one had come to get her, she began to worry that maybe she had been forgotten. The guards said they had no information about what was going on, which only served to make Abby more anxious. By the time lunch was brought to her cell, she was almost frantic.

At three-thirty she was told she had a visitor, and was escorted to a small room by two guards. An exhausted looking Smileowitz was waiting for her.

"What's going on?" She demanded.

"Gwen Mason got the shit beaten out of her last night."

"What?"

"Someone broke into the house in Barbados and worked her over with a baseball bat."

Abby was stunned. "Is she okay?"

"She has a fractured skull. They airlifted her to Miami this morning. She's in surgery."

"Oh my God." Abby might not like Gwen Mason, but she didn't wish the woman any harm.

Smileowitz told Abby that Gwen's father was howling for blood. Lawton Mason had apparently called half the U.S. Senate that morning and the DA's office was trying to placate him.

"They asked the judge to delay our hearing while they investigate. I think they're a little overwhelmed. The Feds are sniffing around, too."

Abby's mind was racing. "The Feds? They think this was Frankie Quarters?"

"I'm sure they do. They probably think Gwen still owed him money. It's not exactly public knowledge that her debts were settled."

"And a baseball bat? That doesn't even make sense. Emily barely had a bruise on her."

Smileowitz nodded. "It doesn't add up. From what my guys tell me, Frankie had nothing to do with this."

"Then who? Boyle?"

"That would be my guess."

"You really think Thomas would do something like this?" Abby asked.

"I think our questions are starting to make some people very uncomfortable. If we're right, the Boyles sent a man to prison for a decade to cover up this HHT stuff. You think Thomas wouldn't have someone else take a beating to keep their secret safe?"

JERRY WAS BACK ON duty that evening and he and Abby watched the news together again. Gwen Mason was the top story everywhere. According to the reports, she was out of surgery but still unconscious. Her doctors didn't seem overly optimistic.

The media was in full-blown, out-of-breath, pulse-racing, check-the-facts-later mode. Reporters were scrambling to air with stories that Gwen Mason had been dealing drugs and owed money to Frankie Quarters. Others said she was a government informant. One suggested she and Bennett Gardner were romantically involved.

Unconfirmed reports had Frankie being taken in for questioning, but the police and district attorney refused comment. A spokesman for Lawton Mason speculated that the authorities might have been wasting their time chasing after Bennett Gardner while Emily Boyle's real killer was still out there, waiting to strike again.

"American Magazine" ran a couple of promos during the five o'clock news touting anchorwoman Joely Rogan's upcoming interview with Thomas Boyle. Abby begged Jerry to let her watch it, hoping Joely would ask Boyle about the medical records. Jerry agreed only after Abby had promised him Markham's autograph, and a "Journal" sweatshirt.

THOMAS BOYLE'S LATEST interview with "American Magazine" took place in his attorney's law-book-lined office. The location conveyed far more authority than his Georgetown living room. It didn't shock Abby when Boyle admitted to Joely Rogan that the assault on Gwen Mason raised some troubling questions. She was astonished, however, when he told her that Gwen and Bennett may have both been involved with Emily's murder.

"So you are still convinced Bennett Gardner killed your sister?" Joely wore eyeglasses for the interview, which seemed to add a level of gravity to her questions.

"I am quite sure Bennett Gardner is the man responsible for my sister's death. But the attack on Gwen Mason raises certain questions regarding who actually struck the fatal blows."

"How so?"

"Mr. Gardner has a well-documented history of trouble with drugs, alcohol and the law, as does Ms. Mason. People who exist in that world run with a dangerous crowd. New evidence has come to light indicating that Gwen Mason owed a great deal of money to a drug dealer, an extremely violent felon. I can't help wondering if Bennett Gardner was somehow connected to this particular dealer as well. It wouldn't shock me to find out that both Bennett Gardner and Gwen Mason were responsible for the brutal murder of my sister."

"So you think Gwen Mason helped Bennett Gardner murder your sister?"

"Not intentionally. But the authorities believe she may have played a role. New evidence, that I personally am not at liberty to discuss, seems to indicate that the recent violent attack on Gwen Mason is connected to my sister's murder."

"Do you think whoever killed Emily may have been looking for Gwen?" Joely Rogan asked.

"It's possible," Boyle said.

"But wouldn't that exonerate Bennett Gardner?"

Boyle ran a hand through his hair. "No, not at all. Bennett Gardner may not have assaulted Gwen Mason himself, but that doesn't mean he isn't involved. Police and prosecutors are beginning to suspect he might be part of a larger conspiracy."

Conspiracy my ass, Abby thought. What kind pathetic excuse for an interview was this? She was disgusted that a journalist of Joely Rogan's caliber wasn't pressing Boyle harder about his answers. She didn't even attempt to question him about his family's medical records. HHT was never mentioned. Rogan had the opportunity to ask him point blank if there was a family history of the condition, but she didn't even bring it up. Abby was positive that this must have been a condition of him agreeing to the interview. Joely Rogan gets the big story, "American Magazine" gets monster ratings, and Thomas Boyle gets to spin his version of the latest developments in the case without having to answer any unpleasant, probing questions about his family's medical history.

"WE ARE GOING back to court today, aren't we?" Abby asked Smileowitz when he came to see her the next morning.

"I wouldn't count on it. The D.A. asked for another day. They're still tripping over themselves trying to figure out this Gwen Mason thing."

"And the judge gave it to them? How long can she keep me locked up?"

"As long as she wants, unless you've changed your mind about revealing your source on the medical file."

Abby crossed her arms. "Not likely."

"Then just sit tight. Things are moving along."

"Oh yeah?"

"Yeah. Lawton Mason saw Boyle's interview last night and went berserk."

"Can you blame him?"

"Not at all. If that was my daughter that asshole was throwing accusations at I'd take a freaking baseball bat to *his* head."

"What about Frankie Quarters?"

"The cops picked him up, but he had nothing to do with this crap."

"So what are we going to do?"

"We? You're going to remain here. I'm meeting with one of Lawton Mason's lawyers at noon."

"You called them?"

"They called me. I think they might have an interest in our little theory."

THE NEWS THAT evening was more of the same. All of the reports focused on Gwen Mason's condition and the hunt for her baseball-bat-wielding attacker. Gwen's doctors appeared very uncomfortable answering questions at a hospital press conference. Despite the reporters' best efforts, none of the physicians would make any sort of prognosis regarding Gwen's recovery. All said it was much too early to tell. Abby took this to be a bad sign.

Most of the news programs also had correspondents reporting from Barbados, where no new information had been uncovered. Not one report mentioned HHT.

Abby was so angry she didn't think she'd ever get to sleep that night, but eventually she nodded off. Even alone in a jail cell, though, she wasn't going to get any rest.

"Ms. Gardner?" a soft female voice asked.

Abby opened her eyes briefly and thought she saw a young woman standing outside her cell. She figured she must be dreaming and rolled over.

"Ms. Gardner, please wake up."

Abby rolled back over and opened her eyes. She wasn't dreaming. There *was* a woman standing outside her cell calling her name. Abby's vision was still blurred from sleep, but it appeared to be Emily Boyle.

"I need to speak with you."

"What the hell?" Abby sat up on her cot. She looked at the young woman gripping the bars of her cell, and she truthfully couldn't believe her eyes.

It was Cassandra Boyle.

"How did you get in here?" Abby demanded.

"I got some help from a friend. I need to speak with you."

"Yeah, well, I have a few things I'd like to go over with you, too."

Cassandra Boyle looked so much like her sister Emily that the two could have been twins. Cassandra rolled Jerry's chair over from his desk and sat down outside of Abby's cell. She looked around uneasily as she spoke, her eyes moving from the cell's bars to the ceiling to her hands.

"I normally try to keep as much distance between my brother and myself as possible," she explained. "My sister tried to do the same. Politics is Thomas's thing. Actually, it's the family thing, but Thomas sees it as his legacy and I respect that." Cassandra shifted uneasily in her seat. "You must understand that I was very young when my parents and my brother died. I never knew any of them. Thomas and Emily were all I had." Abby noticed that Cassandra's voice caught the same way Bennett's did when he said Emily's name. "I love Thomas, and now he is all I have left. I don't campaign for him, I don't go to his parties, and I make a point to keep a low profile. All the time, however, trying to be a good Boyle."

"Then what are you doing here?"

"I heard about your court hearing, and I caught some of my brother's performance on the news. It made me ill."

"You too?" Abby asked.

Cassandra cleared her throat. "Then I heard about Gwen Mason. I'm hoping that what happened to her is just a terrible coincidence."

Abby rolled her eyes. "Yeah, I'm sure that's just a big coincidence."

"In any case, this has gone way too far."

"What's gone way too far?"

"I've spent the last few hours desperately trying to figure out how to save your brother without destroying mine, but I couldn't come up with an answer."

"Then why are you here?"

Cassandra looked at Abby. "I can't just sit by and watch them do to Bennett what they did to that poor mailman after Gilbert died. Emily loved Bennett and I loved my sister. I know she wouldn't want this to happen to him. You're right about the HHT."

Abby dug her fingernails into her hand to keep from smiling.

"My mother had it, Gilbert had it, Emily had it and I have it. Thomas is the only one of us who didn't inherit it."

"I'm sorry," Abby said.

"I am, too. I'm going to speak to the judge in the morning."

THIRTY-ONE

ABBY NEVER GOT back to sleep that night. She couldn't wait for court to begin the next day.

She had begged Cassandra to call Smileowitz after she left the jail and she promised she would.

Abby could barely contain herself as she was escorted into the courtroom. Thomas looked up from his huddle with the district attorney and scowled at her, but his air of confidence quickly turned to confusion when his sister walked into the courtroom, a large envelope tucked under her arm. His entire body seemed to sag when Smileowitz informed Judge Gower that the defense had uncovered a new witness who could prove definitively that Emily Boyle was not murdered.

The courtroom, which was filled with more journalists than should ever be put in one single room, was buzzing. Judge Gower banged her gavel a few times for silence, and then ordered all of the pertinent parties into her chambers. Abby watched Thomas desperately try to make eye contact with his sister, but Cassandra wouldn't meet his glance. She looked as if she was ready to cry.

"What the hell is going on here, Thomas?" A red-faced James Chandler demanded as they were escorted into Judge Gower's chambers. Abby felt sorry for the district attorney. Except for the judge, he was the only one who didn't know the grenade Cassandra Boyle was about to hurl in his general direction.

"I WAS SUSPICIOUS about Emily's death right from the start," Cassandra told Judge Gower. "And I'm sorry I didn't come forward earlier, but I wasn't sure. I knew Emily and Bennett fought a lot, but I didn't think he was the type to hurt anyone."

183

Abby looked at her brother. Bennett was seated in a chair in a corner of the office, flanked by two court officers. He was watching the floor.

"Once I learned how hard Thomas was trying to keep my family's medical records a secret, I knew the HHT had killed Emily, too."

"You son of a bitch," Chandler hissed at Thomas. "You knew about this?"

"Mr. Chandler, if you cannot restrain yourself, I will have you removed from these proceedings."

Chandler simmered as Cassandra continued.

"The HHT came from my mother's side of the family. It killed her the day I was born. There are several physicians who can testify that she, Emily, and Gilbert all suffered from the same disorder. I can put you in touch with them as soon as you'd like."

CASSANDRA HAD BROUGHT her own extensive medical records into court that day for Judge Gower to examine. Her doctors had documented that Cassandra not only suffered from HHT, but that she had inherited the condition from her mother who had died as a result of it. One physician had also noted that her sister and brother suffered from HHT as well.

Judge Gower dismissed the case against Bennett just before three o'clock that afternoon and let Abby off the hook shortly thereafter. Both of the Gardner children were eager to get home and see their father as quickly as possible, but Cassandra requested a few moments alone with them before they left. They spoke in a small room next to the courtroom.

"What about William Radley?" Abby asked Cassandra.

The youngest Boyle chose her words carefully, her voice slightly above a whisper. "I was very young when my brother died, I really don't remember it at all, but I've heard bits and pieces about what happened over the years. From what I've been able to deduce, what happened to Mr. Radley was my grandfather's idea."

"That's just great," Abby said angrily.

Bennett shot his sister a silencing look.

"He thought the disease was some genetic flaw that my mother's family brought into the mix and he was worried it might affect my father's chances for the White House."

Abby crossed her arms. "Well, God forbid the Boyles should lose an election."

"Abby, please," Bennett said.

Abby shook her head. "No, Bennett, these people sent an innocent man to prison for a decade to protect their political aspirations. Your grandfather figured no one would miss a nobody like William Radley, and it would keep the family's image as the perfect people intact."

"What my grandfather did disgusts me," Cassandra said quietly.

"I wouldn't be too proud of what your brother attempted, either."

"Thomas isn't a bad person, but I'm sure he figured if it got out that Emily died from the HHT, it would just be a matter of time before someone made the connection with William Radley."

"So, instead of admitting it, he tried to do the same thing to my brother."

"Bennett is lucky. Your family has a lot more resources than William Radley did."

Abby stood up. "Yeah, well, justice always seems to work out better for the rich, but I certainly don't have to explain that to you."

"Leave her alone, Abby," Bennett snapped. "This hasn't been easy for her, either."

But Abby didn't want to leave her alone. "What about Gwen Mason?"

Cassandra picked at the arm of her chair. "I honestly don't know. I feel sick about what happened to that woman, but I keep hoping it's just a terrible coincidence."

"Coincidence, my ass. You people could care less…"

"Enough, already!" Bennett shouted at his sister. "Leave her alone!" Abby looked at her brother and Cassandra. She realized that she was sitting in a room with the two people in the world who probably loved Emily Boyle the most. They had both grieved for her completely alone, until now.

THIRTY-TWO

"You don't have to stay here with him," Bennett told his sister as they walked along the beach with Maggie one sunny afternoon a week after they were released. "You've done more than your share. I can handle it for a while."

"It's okay. I told Gordon I wanted some more time off before I go back. I want things to settle down a bit."

It was amazing how much had already settled. The media got bored of Bennett's part of the story twenty-four hours after he was released from jail. The press corps was now busy chasing the Boyles.

Thomas Boyle resigned from his position with the Justice Department two days after Bennett was released. The statement released after his departure claimed he had left to pursue "other career options." Abby wasn't surprised that Boyle didn't hold his own press conference, since he had become uncharacteristically but understandably tight-lipped after Cassandra started talking.

Lawton Mason, though, was far from silent. He hadn't shut his mouth in close to eight days. Thankfully, Gwen was out of danger, but she was facing extensive plastic surgery and years of physical therapy. Her father had hired a high-priced team of lawyers and private investigators to look into the assault, and had established a sizeable reward that was guaranteed to bring every imaginable nut job out of the woodwork.

William Radley had retained Smileowitz and Associates to handle his civil case against the Boyles. Smileowitz expected Radley to become the richest laundry driver in the history of Utah.

Abby had made good use of her time since being freed from jail. She had spent an entire morning that week on the phone giving George Pierce's name to every tax agency and active religious recruiter she could think of. It had taken a while for Markham to get her the name, but his associates at the *Weekly Globe* assured him that

George Pierce was the clerk at Harborview General Hospital who sold them the photographs of Abby's father. She was planning on having his telephone and cable disconnected the following day. Then she would report him to the hospital.

"I'm serious," Bennett said. "You really don't have to stay. I'm sure you're dying to get back to your place."

Bennett was doing as well as could be expected since his release. The bruises on his face were almost completely gone. Abby had tried not to mention Emily to him, but Bennett told her he liked talking about her. Cassandra had been out to see him twice. They seemed to be helping each other cope.

"I owe you more than I'll ever be able to repay, Abby. The least I can do is spring you from this place."

It was strange, but Abby was in no hurry to leave. It was the first time she could recall that she actually enjoyed being around her father and her brother. Later that week, she was planning on driving with Danny Morello to D.C. They were going to move him into his new law school digs, and then take off for the beach for a few days before his classes began. Then she would go back to work.

"It's really okay," she insisted. "It isn't that bad here."

Bennett started examining Abby's head. "I'm checking for some sort of brain injury."

"I know it's odd," she said, swatting him away. "I'd always figured I would gnaw off my own thumb before I agreed to stay here without being under house arrest or in some sort of hypnotic trance. But you know I'm considering maybe hanging out with you and the old man for a while longer."

Bennett put an arm around his sister's shoulder. "Hey, it's fine with me, but you'll have to clear it with The Doctor, you know. Get his okay."

"I'll talk to him about it at dinner."

"Good."

"I understand we're doing 'West Side Story.'"

Lisa M. Tillman is a veteran television writer and producer, whose work has appeared on Fox, Court TV and The History Channel. Born and raised in New York, she is a graduate of New York University's Tisch School of the Arts. She spent a decade bouncing around Southern New England, and now makes her home in Maryland, where she lives with her husband, two children and dog.